HO HO HORROR

Edited by

STEVE ROSSITER

auslit.net

The Australian Literature Review

Ho Ho Horror is a project of The Australian Literature Review (www.auslit.net).

Illustrations and cover art by Andrew McKiernan (www.andrewmckiernan.com).

ISBN: 0987124226
ISBN-13: 9780987124227

CHRISTMAS HORROR FICTION FOR ADULT READERS

DEDICATION

Ho Ho Horror is dedicated to the contributing authors, illustrator and cover artist Andrew McKiernan, and all the other up-and-coming fiction authors in Australia and around the world.

A special mention goes to Gordon Reece, whom I met at the Launch Party for the 2011 Somerset Writers Festival on the Gold Coast, Australia. His short story Ho Ho Ho was the inspiration for *Ho Ho Horror*.

A special mention also goes to contributing authors Belinda Dorio and Sam Stephens whom I will be working with throughout 2012 as they each write their debut novel.

- Editor, Steve Rossiter
(December 2011)

CONTENTS

ILLUSTRATIONS

HO HO HO

GORDON REECE

It was the night before Christmas and Danny Coyle was too excited to sleep. He squeezed his eyes tight shut and lay very, very still, but the black oblivion he yearned for just wouldn't come. He tried his best not to think about the miraculous visit that was fast approaching, but it was no use; his mind kept returning to it again and again, the same way his tongue would keep prodding and probing at a wiggly tooth. He felt the excitement burn in his stomach and his heart was pounding so hard he could actually feel his chest jolt in his pajamas as if Kevin Dixon (who liked to creep up behind you in the playground and punch you on the back) was thumping him over and over again. He wondered if a seven-year-old boy had ever got so excited on Christmas Eve that he'd actually *died*.

Santa was out there somewhere, soaring through the night sky on his magic sleigh, bringing a sack full of gifts to every boy and every girl in the whole wide world. And soon - *soon* - he'd come to Danny's house. He'd guide his reindeer down into Melville Street and land on the roof with a clatter of hooves and a jingling of sleigh bells. He'd find the sack bearing Danny's name on a white card label, then climb on down the chimney and, just as he did every year, carefully lay out all of Danny's presents on the sofa in the lounge. He'd drink the sherry and eat the mince pies mum and dad had left out for him (the reindeer always ate their mince pies too), then he'd creep quietly up the stairs and into Danny's room and leave a stocking filled with little treats at the end of his bed. This overstuffed stocking would be the first thing Danny saw when he woke up on Christmas morning - the hors-d'oeuvre to whet his appetite for the great feast of presents that awaited him downstairs.

Danny was always excited on Christmas Eve, but the reason he was in such an agony of anticipation this year could be explained in just two words: *Lieutenant Danger*. Danny had asked Santa to bring him the new Lieutenant Danger action figure (the one equipped for sub-aqua warfare), the new Lieutenant Danger DVD *Triumph of the Malikons*, and the new Lieutenant Danger annual, but the present he wanted more than anything else on his Christmas list was the Lieutenant Danger Combat Adventure Kit. The Combat Adventure Kit came with a camouflage uniform, water bottle, plastic machete, handgun, spy camera and compass. The very thought of The Combat Adventure Kit sent a feverish paroxysm of longing coursing through Danny's body. Because Danny knew that when he was dressed in the camouflage uniform and had the machete and pistol tucked into his belt, he wouldn't just be playing at Lieutenant Danger anymore - he would *be* Lieutenant Danger.

Lieutenant Danger was a cartoon series that had been launched that spring on TV. Max Danger, the eponymous hero, was a muscular, square-jawed US special forces soldier. While on a secret mission to the jungles of Borneo he'd witnessed the arrival of the Malikons' invasion armada - flesh-eating monsters from outer space intent on brutal conquest. In a wry homage to *Invasion of the Bodysnatchers*, the Malikons were able to turn themselves into perfect replicas of any human being they touched – or rather, *almost* perfect replicas; Malikon impostors could still be identified by their diamond-shaped pupils, their black tongues, and the thick wiry hairs that grew in the palms of their hands - tell-tale features which they couldn't change but could only do their best to disguise.

Lieutenant Danger was never able to convince the US government that the Malikon threat was real. In a piquantly ironic twist, he was seen by the top brass as a paranoid troublemaker and a dangerous loose cannon. And so, week after week, he would perform death-defying heroics to save the United States from the latest Malikon plot and receive only an angry dressing down from the High Command for his pains. Most episodes ended with General Prendergast, the Lieutenant's bete noir, blustering, 'there's no such things as Malikons, Lieutenant Danger! It's all in your mind!"

From the very first episode Danny had been hooked, and now every Saturday morning found him sitting cross-legged on the floor in front of the TV waiting impatiently for *Lieutenant Danger* to start. Danny was a boisterous, hyperactive little boy who could rarely sit still for long, but during the half hour that *Lieutenant Danger* ran he didn't move a muscle. He would stare fixedly at the screen, his mouth hanging open in awe, spit bubbles forming and popping on his lips. Not even lollies could break the spell the show cast over him, and a chocolate bar would remain melting in limp fingers quite forgotten. Even when it finished, he didn't immediately rush off to play, but carried on sitting there as if turning over in his mind all the subtle implications of what he'd just seen.

Danny had been bitten by crazes before – basketball, WWF wrestling, Transformers - but this was on a different scale altogether. Danny became totally *obsessed* by Lieutenant Danger; he thought about little else, he talked about little else, he cared about little else. At school, no matter what subject the teacher gave the class for a story, Danny would always find a way - sometimes with incredible ingenuity - to write Lieutenant Max Danger and the Malikons into the action. And it was the same in Art class. When school broke up for Christmas and he brought home the paintings he'd done that term, every one featured Max Danger shooting or stabbing a Malikon. Even the one entitled *My Day at the Zoo* had a bloody struggle going on around the elephant enclosure, Max Danger cutting off a Malikon's head with his jungle machete. His parents seized on one, that old staple of the primary school art teacher, *My Family*, which miraculously seemed to have escaped the Max Danger treatment - until, that is, they noticed the diamond-shaped pupils in Danny's dad's eyes and the tell-tale hairs growing out of the palms of his hands.

His parents weren't unduly concerned about Danny's obsession however. Danny was their only child and in their eyes he could do no wrong. They doted on him and overindulged him and there were doughy rolls of fat on his belly and sugar decay in his teeth because 'no' wasn't a word they could often bring themselves to say to him. So while Danny's mum feigned concern as she discussed Lieutenant Danger with the other mums over coffee, she was secretly proud of the all-consuming, blinkered focus Danny displayed in his enthusiasm. Hadn't Einstein, hadn't all the great geniuses, in fact, shown a similar almost autistic monomania? Wasn't this in reality an early sign of the mental distinction that would see Danny emerge in adulthood as an exceptional individual?

Danny's dad was similarly sanguine, but for different reasons. Although he couldn't admit it in front of his wife's PC friends (some of whom were so anti gender stereo-typing they encouraged their sons to play with dolls and to bake cupcakes), he was actually delighted to see Danny obsessed by something so unmistakably male, not to say *macho* as Lieutenant Danger. It gave him a real thrill of fatherly pride to see his son - his *boy* - running around the house, his face smeared with camouflage paint, pretending to kick the shit out of the Malikons. Of course it could be awkward when Danny got carried away and played a bit too rough with one of the other kids (something which tended to happen quite often these days he had to admit), but he'd rather that than risk Danny growing up a faggot.

So they were both loathe to discourage Danny's obsession with Lieutenant Danger, and when he begged them for a Lieutenant Danger bed set or computer game or backpack or T-shirt they dutifully bought it for him.

Of all the Lieutenant Danger spin-offs that flooded the shops, Danny liked the action figures best of all. There were three of them: Lieutenant Danger equipped for snow warfare, jungle warfare and desert warfare and they each came with an array of miniature plastic accessories - daggers, ninja death stars, handcuffs, grenades, sniper rifles and machine guns – all of them guaranteed to thrill bellicose little boys. Danny, it went without saying, was the proud owner of all three.

Danny played with his Lieutenant Danger action figures with an intensity his parents had never seen him show in his play before. Hour after hour he'd wander around the house holding one of the little plastic mannequins in his hand, its head twisted sharply to the side, its articulated arms bent at strange angles. And all the while he'd be talking inaudibly to himself, absorbedly narrating the adventure he was acting out. They watched him trotting in and out of the garden, his lips moving rapidly, his brow sternly furrowed and agreed that such a rich, self-contained imagination was a healthy sign in a child.

If they'd been able to hear what Danny was actually saying to himself however, it's doubtful they would have felt quite so at ease.....

Danny's games, you see, nearly always followed the same pattern: Lieutenant Danger would unwittingly walk into a Malikon ambush, and after a protracted, bloody battle the flesh-eating villains would capture him alive. They'd take their prisoner back to their secret lair - a rat-infested sewer beneath the Abandoned City - and, in a specially constructed escape-proof chamber, they'd slowly, lovingly, torture him to death. The variety of tortures Danny devised for him really did show a highly developed imagination. He ran the hot tap until it was scalding and then held Lieutenant Danger's face under the torrent until all the flesh had boiled white and sloughed off in chunks; he buried him alive in the mud and placed a heavy rock on top so that he wouldn't be able to claw his way to the surface; with a cigarette lighter left behind by an uncle and never missed, he burned his hands until the fingers turned black and curled back on themselves; he dropped him from his bedroom window onto the concrete patio below until every bone in his body was broken and he'd never be able to walk again; but most delicious of all was when he tied a piece of electric cable around Lieutenant Danger's neck and pulled and pulled with all his might. Danny's cherubic face would flush deep red and his pee-pee would grow achingly stiff as the Special Forces hero writhed in excruciating agony.

It was no good. Sleep still wouldn't come. And now, to make matters worse, Danny needed to go to the bathroom. Desperately. He sat up and groped around in the darkness, but no stocking had miraculously appeared while he'd been tossing and turning beneath his Lieutenant Danger duvet.

Danny slept in a bunk bed - another whim his parents had indulged him in - even though he had no brother or sister to share it. He always slept in the top bunk; he felt it added something adventurous, something military to the prosaic routine of going to bed. Now he crawled on all fours to the end of his bunk, and, with practiced ease, clambered over the bedstead and held himself there momentarily until his feet were firmly planted on a rung of the wooden ladder. It was from this position, when he woke up feeling particularly energetic, that he'd throw himself into the air, catch hold of the basketball hoop his dad had fixed to the wall for him, dangle there for as long as he could bear it, and then drop to the floor like Lieutenant Danger parachuting into action. He didn't think of doing that now, however. It was too dark and he needed to pee *badly*.

He put on his Lieutenant Danger dressing-gown and tiptoed out onto the landing. It didn't feel right to be awake at this time of night on Christmas Eve. Danny felt sure it could only bring bad luck. He might bump into Santa Claus bringing his stocking up to his room, and Santa might get mad and decide to take back all the presents he'd brought for him. He might take back the Lieutenant Danger Combat Adventure Kit, and then Danny wouldn't be able to dress up in the camouflage uniform and run around the house with the machete and the pistol tucked in his belt hunting down the Malikons and cutting off their heads. Danny couldn't bear to think about it and determined to get to the bathroom and back as quickly and as quietly as he could, before anything bad happened.

Danny peed without turning the lights on and tried to keep his stream trained on the sides of the ceramic bowl and out of the water so that no one would hear him. His dad was working the night shift at the saw mill as he did every Christmas Eve, but his mum was still up, and he could hear the muted chatter of the TV set coming from the lounge-room. Without thinking, Danny almost flushed, but he caught himself just in time.

He was almost back at his room when a sharp scream from downstairs pierced the quiet of the house. Danny froze in mid-step as if caught in a powerful searchlight, and, holding his breath, his eyes huge and unblinking, he strained his ears to listen. A few seconds later, another sound reached him, not a scream this time, more like a moan of pain. Then it came again and again and again, gradually finding its own frenetic rhythm like the urgent beating of a fevered pulse.

Danny crept towards the top of the stairs and noiselessly descended the first five steps. Craning his neck, he peered through the wrought iron balustrade and tried to see into the kitchen.

He didn't understand what he was looking at initially; some sort of creature with four arms and four legs was flailing around on the floor by the sink in its death throes. Danny recoiled as if he'd lifted a large stone in the garden and found its underside crawling with earwigs. When he looked again, however, he slowly began to understand what it was: two people lay knotted together, writhing against one another in a desperate struggle. One of them was unmistakably his mum. She lay on her back with her bare legs raised, her hair a fiery auburn starburst across the black and yellow lino. A man was on top of her, his naked, mushroom-white buttocks pumping up and down, the muscles clenching and unclenching with every thrust, and with every thrust his mum let out that cry of agony. And although Danny couldn't see the man's face clearly, there was no doubting who it was - the cascading white beard, the red hat with the white trimming, the red tunic with the thick black belt round the middle - the man doing this filthy thing to his mum, the man who was making her cry out in pain, was none other than Santa Claus himself!

Danny hurried back to his bedroom, the graphic image burned indelibly into his retina. He climbed up to the top bunk as quickly as he could, not even pausing to take off his dressing-gown, burrowed deep beneath his Lieutenant Danger duvet and lay there without moving, his heart racing. It was a long time before he was calm enough to try to figure out what it could all mean.

He'd heard bigger boys talk about this at school. He was pretty sure this was what they called 'shagging' and he was pretty sure that 'shagging' had something to do with the 'f' word but he didn't know what exactly. This 'shagging' was what mums and dads did together, this was how they made babies. But Santa Claus wasn't Danny's dad. Danny's dad was at work in the saw mill. Santa Claus had no right to shag his mum. Only Danny's dad was allowed to do it; that was the rule. And his mum hadn't wanted Santa to do it to her. That was why she'd been crying out in pain. That was why she'd been clawing at his back with her long nails. As Danny well knew, you only used your nails against someone when you really, really wanted to hurt them.

It seemed to Danny that if Santa Claus could do this to his mum then people had got Santa all wrong. He wasn't a nice man at all. He was a bad man. A very, very bad man indeed. Or what if..... a devastating thought struck Danny and he sat up abruptly in bed: what if the Santa he'd seen downstairs in the kitchen wasn't the *real* Santa at all? What if this Santa was really a Malikon who'd shaved his palms, dyed his black tongue red and put contact lenses in his eyes? What if he'd tricked his mum into letting him into the house and then forced her to do that disgusting thing? And any minute now this impostor Santa would start to climb the stairs and slowly make his way towards Danny's bedroom...

What should he do? Danny thought with rising panic. *What should he do?* But then he realized that this was actually the wrong question; the question he should have been asking was: *What would Lieutenant Danger do?*

When he'd finished making love to his wife, Danny's dad kissed her playfully on the tip of her nose, got unsteadily to his feet and yanked up his red Santa trousers. She stayed stretched out on the kitchen floor enjoying the post-coital afterglow and the weird thrill of being naked and splay-legged in a room where she'd only ever been clothed and busy and strangely de-sexed before.

"Santa comes but once a year…." he grinned, adjusting the false beard that had managed to work its way round to his ear.

"Mmmm, but it's sure worth waiting for," she purred.

They were both pretty drunk and they giggled like mischievous children at their own naughtiness.

When the senior manager had looked at him around midnight, told him he looked like shit and sent him home, Danny's dad hadn't argued. Before heading off he'd stopped in at the warehouse to drink some 'medicinal' scotch with some of the boys there and that's when he'd seen Bob Holden in the Santa suit. Bob had been working as Santa at a department store in town for a bit of extra Christmas cash and had come to work at the mill still wearing his costume for a joke. The moment he'd seen it he'd thought of Danny and how thrilled he'd be to get a visit from the great man himself. He'd asked Bob if he could borrow it and Bob had said that as long as he had the suit back for when the store reopened on Boxing Day, it was 'no problemo'.

On the short drive home, no doubt influenced by the three scotches he'd had, he decided to change into the Santa suit in the car port, creep into the house and give his wife a surprise. As it turned out he found her half-cut on Chardonnay and as horny as hell, and *he* was the one who'd ended up getting the surprise.

"I'm gonna take Danny's stocking up now," he said, rearranging his pants so that his erection didn't show.

She sat up and scratched her scalp vigorously with both hands, and her breasts, heavy and matronly in her thirty-eighth year, jiggled. She felt a little ridiculous now sitting naked in the middle of the kitchen and reached for her balled up night gown.

"His stocking's on the recliner in the lounge-room," she said. "Don't touch anything on the sofa, I've set it all up so that the Combat Adventure Kit is the first thing he'll see."

Danny's dad tugged down the black plastic belt which had ridden up almost to his nipples, and looked at her with a grin whose boyish excitement was still clearly discernible through the cloud of synthetic white beard.

"God, he'll be so rapt when he sees 'Santa' bringing him his stocking!"

She'd rolled the nightshirt down over her nakedness now and was trying unsuccessfully to light a cigarette by the sink with an exhausted zippo lighter. She looked back at him over her shoulder.

"You're not going to wake him up are you?"

"Why not?" he shrugged. "It'll make his Christmas!"

"You'll excite him too much – he'll never get back to sleep! - you know how he gets. You can put the Santa suit on for him tomorrow – that'll be good enough."

Danny's dad shifted his weight uncomfortably, trying to hide his disappointment. He'd been looking forward to playing Santa for Danny.

She came over to him and nuzzled at his neck and he automatically cupped one of her breasts.

"We need to get some rest, sweetie," she crooned wearily. "Danny'll be jumping on our bed in a few hours as it is. It was half four last year! *Please* don't wake him up."

"Alright," he conceded reluctantly. "But I might as well keep it on – you know, just in case he wakes up anyway."

She looked up at him and narrowed her eyes.

"I won't wake him up! I promise!"

Slowly she disentangled herself from him and started to make a pot of tea to take up to bed. Then she paused.

"What will you say to him if he does wake up?"

Danny's dad thought for a moment and then smiled.

"Ho, ho, ho, of course! What else?"

Danny's bedroom door was tight against the carpet nap and usually when his dad went to check on him last thing at night he entered slowly in case the loud shushing should wake him. Tonight however, he pushed the door open forcefully, half hoping it would. He stood there for a moment and waited, but no rustling of the duvet, no sleepy voice came from the bunk bed in the far corner. Disappointed, he started to make his way slowly across the room nursing the stocking in his arms. He went cautiously, sliding one foot out in front of the other like a slow motion skater as the glow of light from the landing only frayed the edges of the darkness, and he didn't want to tread on a toy in the gloom and turn his ankle over – been there done that, as he was fond of saying.

He found the wooden ladder hanging at the foot of the top bunk and climbed up the first two rungs with some effort. He took the stocking, which was stuffed so tight with chocolate bars and comic books that it felt like a fully inflated foot ball, and lay it gently at Danny's feet. He didn't descend at once. He lingered there, letting his eyes grow accustomed to the darkness until he could make out quite clearly the hump in the duvet where his little boy lay snuggled up fast asleep. In spite of his promise to his wife he was sorely tempted to wake him. He knew it would give Danny the thrill of his life – he'd be talking about it all the way through to next Christmas! It seemed a crying shame to pass up such a great opportunity; he'd probably never get his hands on such a picture perfect Santa suit again. It would be different tomorrow in the bright light of day. Danny was so sharp he'd most likely see through his disguise straightaway. But if he were to wake up now, and catch a bleary impression of Santa, that would be perfect. That would be just perfect.

His wife was probably right of course. Most likely Danny would be too excited to go back to sleep and he'd be in their room long before dawn showing them everything in his stocking and pleading with them to get up so that he could go downstairs and see what 'big presents' Santa had brought him. But although he knew how rough he'd feel all the next day with so little sleep, there was a part of him that didn't care. The buzz he got when he saw Danny really happy easily outweighed all the negatives spoiling him so often brought in its wake, and it always had.

He started to reach out his hand towards the duvet, but just as it was about to alight on an image of Lieutenant Danger kung-fu kicking a Malikon in the head, he hesitated. He was overcome by the deep, atavistic taboo against waking a sleeping child, and even though he desperately wanted to, he just couldn't bring himself to do it.

He lightly placed his fingers where he imagined the seven-year-old's little feet lay, and whispered softly, "Sweet dreams, son." When Danny sprang out at him from under the duvet and looped the belt of his dressing-gown over his head, the shock sent him reeling backwards into empty space. In the nanosecond he was in mid-air he braced for a painful impact....but that impact never came; his entire weight was caught instead by the homemade noose Danny had double-knotted to the basketball hoop. The sickening jolt was so brutal it forced his teeth deep into the raw meat of his tongue and jerked his body violently back towards the bunk bed. It wasn't quite enough to break his neck, however, and he dangled there, wriggling like a fish on a hook, desperately scrabbling at the toweling garrote choking off his air supply, his eyes bulging, his lips blowing obscene blood bubbles, his feet frantically kicking out for the floor which remained out of reach.

With deadly black flowers bursting into bloom across his vision, he despairingly thrust out his left leg and managed to catch hold of the bottom rung of the ladder. Pushing himself back against the wall he was able to get a hand to the bedstead, and the agonising pain in his neck eased long enough for him to suck down a lungful of precious air. And then he was aware of Danny again, slipping under the guard rail and dropping to the floor, coming towards him with purposeful malice, a small Phillips screwdriver glinting in his right hand. He felt a searing pain in his calf muscle and his foot slipped off the rung, he lost his grip on the bedstead and the choking agony began again. He watched with horrified disbelief as Danny carefully unhooked the ladder, dragged it out of his reach and lay it on the floor. He blacked out for several seconds and when he regained consciousness he was dully aware of Danny swinging on his legs.

The only hope, he thought, as his eyes rolled slowly up into his head, was if the backboard came away from the wall under his weight. But then he remembered the doting meticulousness with which he'd put it up – *no botch job for Danny! Nothing but the best for Danny!* He remembered the twelve industrial-strength screws he'd drilled into the wall to secure the backboard firmly into place so that Danny could shoot baskets in his bedroom. That backboard was never going to give way…

When the impostor Santa had finally stopped twitching, Lieutenant Danger let go of his legs and switched on his bedroom light. He put the ladder back in place and climbed up so that he'd be able to reach the Malikon's face, holding the screwdriver tightly in his hand so that he wouldn't drop it.

LIEUTEN
DAN
U.S. SPECIAL FO

'Now,' he thought, 'to scratch out those contact lenses and reveal the diamond-shaped pupils underneath.....'

LET IT SNOW

SAM STEPHENS

Trees crowded the small dirt road and raked their spindly branches down the panels of Jake Wellman's overpriced, under-performing SUV. He cringed with every screech and scrape.

His wife rolled her eyes.

"Settle down, it's only a few branches."

"Don't tell me to settle down, Katherine."

His voice was sharper than he had intended, but wasn't really in the mood to apologise.

"It's Christmas, Jake."

Like that was supposed to mean something.

The hotel came into view, saving him from what could extend into quite a long nag session.

"Here we are," he muttered.

There was a bare patch of dirt to the side of the track. He guessed that it was meant to be the car park, and he pulled in and killed the engine.

Stepping out, he breathed in the forest air. It was a little humid and smelled a bit like rotting fungus. Whoever described country air as fresh had obviously never been to the country. He chided himself. This was meant to be a holiday--time to leave the stress of his failing business behind and enjoy some time with his wife and kids.

Three doors slammed shut. Sari and Michael came up behind him. At nine and eleven they were grasping for teenage attitude already, and had decided that hanging with dad wasn't as cool as it used to be. So when then both slipped an arm around his waist it surprised him. He returned the hug. Katherine rounded the car and smiled at their little group. Beautiful. Perfect.

Michael shoved Sari's arm aside.

"Don't touch my arm," he said.

Sari shoved back, and then it was on.

Well beauty and perfection can't last forever, right?

"Kids, stop it," Katherine said.

"Come on, let's go find out which cabin is ours," Jake said and started walking toward the hotel without waiting for a response.

The hotel almost faded into the background of thick pines and shrubs. It was built probably from these same pines; a wooden cabin but on a mansion scale. Wide steps led into the foyer, and Jake ran his palm over the polished wooded railing as he climbed. It was actually quite charming.

The hotel door was adorned with a green plastic Christmas wreath, and red tinsel was strung above the door in long arcs.

He pushed open the door and was hit by a beautiful wave of cool, dry air. Bless the person that invented air conditioning.

A man stood at reception, palms flat on the counter, and a smile so wide Jake half expected his cheeks to split open. Either that or the man's jaw would dislocate and he'd swallow them whole.

"And you must be the Wellmans," he said.

"Must I?" Jake asked. "Because if there are any other options..."

The man cast a glance over Jake's shoulder at his still squabbling kids currently being refereed by his wife who seemed to be losing the battle. The man laughed a little too loudly, and then winked. What he was winking about, Jake had no idea. But he offered a smile and pulled out his credit card.

"Thank you sir," the man said and ran the card through the old fashioned credit card imprint machine before handing it back. "Consider yourself checked in. Now, I'm Duncan Mackay, and I'm the owner here. If you need anything, don't hesitate to call me on the phone from your cabin. Your mobile phone won't work out here, but the landline is fine."

"Thank you." Jake reached for the cabin key, though Duncan held onto it tightly. He nodded towards Jake's family.

"If you need *anything* at all," he said, "just call."

Jake looked at him with confusion. Was this some kind of country talk that he didn't understand?

Duncan released the key and then indicated downwards with his eyes. He tipped a statue of a bear to the side and in a hollowed out cavity were several small bags of white power.

"Is that coke?" Jake asked before slapping his mouth quickly shut. He looked around, but luckily there were no other guests.

Duncan gave Jake a scolding frown.

"Yes," Duncan said loud enough. "We have Coke, lemonade, water. All sorts of cold drinks."

Then he winked again. Jake fought an urge to roll his eyes.

"I'll be right," Jake said. "I've got some beers in the car."

Duncan nodded. "Sure thing, but if you change your mind, let me know. Special rates for special customers."

Jake offered an awkward smile.

"We should get unpacked."

"Of course," Duncan said. He took out a map and pointed out their cabin. "This is where you'll be staying. Number four. Beautiful view from there."

"View of what?"

Duncan looked at him like he was a little slow.

"Of the trees, of course."

"Of course," Jake agreed. He was skeptical how overlooking trees in the middle of a forest constituted a view.

"Looks like it's pretty far out," Jake said.

"Sure is," Duncan said with pride. "All our cabins are fully secluded, offering the most relaxing and private stays in the state."

"You should put that on your brochure," Jake joked.

Duncan smiled and tapped a stack of glossy pamphlets on the counter top. And there it was, word for word.

Jake knew if he stayed any longer the battle not to roll his eyes would be lost, and so he smiled, thanked Duncan, and ushered his family out the door.

"Remember Jake," Duncan called out. "Let me know if there is anything I can get you. And Merry Christmas!"

The door swung shut, and after the relative cool of the reception area, the humidity closed around him like a sticky shroud.

Jake checked the map and looked towards where the cabin should be. A tiny path wound into the trees.

"No vehicle access," he said.

“That’s okay,” Katherine said, “After the drive I can do with stretching my legs a little. Same with the kids. Let them work off some energy.”

“But I’m already tired,” Michael said.

“So am I,” Sari said.

“Don’t copy.”

“Don’t you copy.”

“Kids,” Katherine interrupted. “Grab a bag each, and let’s go pick our rooms.”

Jake unloaded a few of the lighter items, and handed them over.

“Meet you down there,” Katherine said and offered a smile. “This’ll be fun. You’ll see.”

Jake returned her smile, though it fell from his face as soon as she turned towards the path to the cabins. Fun? He doubted it. He was just hoping to survive it with his sanity intact. These days he didn’t set the bar of expectation too high.

He was about to grab his bag, but spied the Esky. Why the hell not?

It was buried under several bags, but he managed to crack the lid enough to slip his hand inside. The ice was still frozen, and the beer wonderfully cold. He grabbed a bottle and pulled it free. He twisted the top and took a long sip. Heaven in a bottle. He sat on the back of the car and took another drink. And another. He looked around at the trees, and for just a moment enjoyed the silence. Maybe this holiday would turn out okay after all.

The bottle was empty all too quickly, and Jake sighed. He slipped the empty back into the Esky and surveyed the bags. He took out a few items, stacked them on top of the Esky and picked up the whole load.

The track leading to the cabin was plain dirt, and he almost tripped a few times on tree roots. The branches scraped at his skin. If the trees weren't after his car, they were after him it seemed.

He finally arrived at the cabin. It was perched on the side of a hill, overlooking what was actually quite a nice view. The hill fell into a densely wooded valley, and Jake could feel a gentle breeze drifting up. It wasn't a cool breeze but at least it was movement, and that helped pierce the humidity a little.

He walked up the steps onto the veranda and rested the bags and Esky on the railing while he opened the door of the cabin. Unlike the reception area, there was no rush of cool air.

"Can you turn the air conditioning on?" he called inside.

"I'm trying," Katherine called back. "Hey kids, don't run in here."

Sari came sprinting through the cabin as fast as her nine year old legs would carry her. Michael was close behind. Sari held her brother's phone in the air. Fighting over video games on the phone. What a surprise. He stepped to the side and let them run out of the cabin.

Glass exploded, and Jake snapped his head to the sound. In the time it took to turn his head he already saw in his mind the bleeding faces of his kids and the broken glass of the cabin door. But instead they both stood rigid, their eyes locked on his. The cabin door was still in one piece. So what broke?

“Oh shit,” Jake muttered.

“What happened?” Katherine called out as she hurried towards them.

“Sorry dad,” Michael said. “It was Sari.”

“Was not,” Sari said.

“Stop it,” Jake snapped and they both fell silent.

He looked over the railing at the shattered remains of his beer. The Esky lid lay open, broken glass and foam soaked into the leaves and twigs.

He fought the urge to yell. It was only beer.

Only his lifeline to sanity.

“Oh honey,” Katherine said. “Maybe you can pop into town for some more?”

“A two hour drive to the closest town isn’t really *popping in*.”

Katherine remained silent.

“I’ll help you pick it up,” she finally said.

No bottles had survived, and Jake and Katherine piled the shattered remains into the Esky. They picked up as much as they could fine. Jake took a look around.

“I think that’s all of it,” he said.

Katherine rubbed his back and smiled at him.

“It’ll be okay,” she said.

He nodded.

“I’ll take this up to Duncan and see if he’s got a bin.”

“He’s a strange one.”

“Sure is.” Jake remembered the little bags of cocaine. “He sure is.”

As Jake started the long walk back, Katherine called after him: “Ask Duncan about the air conditioning. I can’t get it to turn on.”

“Yep.”

And then the trees closed behind him. Jake was alone in the forest with just his thoughts. What a way to start the Christmas holidays: overbearing humidity and no beer.

He thought about all the Christmas movies he’d ever seen. Cold snow and warm eggnog. He wondered if that was really how Americans spent their Christmas holidays or if that was just a Hollywood interpretation.

He’d kill for a bit of snow right now. And just one sip of eggnog, whatever the fuck that was.

By the time he made it back to reception, his shirt clung to his sweaty back and neck. He took a discreet sniff of his armpit. It wasn’t a field of roses but it shouldn’t cause anyone to vomit.

The cool of the reception area washed over him, and he briefly considered finding a chair and passing out in the waiting area.

“Hey Jake!” Duncan’s chirpy voice made him think of an over-eager puppy dog, begging to please.

“Hey Duncan,” Jake said. He held up the esky of broken glass and gave it a shake. The shards tinkled inside. “Got a bin?”

Duncan frowned.

“Sure thing, but you should have one in your room. Did you need me to bring one down?”

“No, no that’s okay. Just had a little accident. It’s a whole heap of broken glass, and don’t really want it around the kids. I was hoping I could drop it into your collection bin.”

Duncan skirted the counter and lifted the lid on the esky. He surveyed the mess, shaking his head.

“What a terrible waste of good beer.”

Jake chuckled. Maybe Duncan was alright after all.

“Sure is. It’s like losing a child. A case of children.”

Duncan laughed. “Ice-cold, delicious children with a layer of frost. Hey, come through my office. The bin is out back.”

Jake made his farewell to the beers that were never meant to be and they returned to the cool interior.

“You know, if you like, I’ve got a replacement,” Duncan said.

Jake’s mouth crinkled into a smile. “You got more beer?”

"Well, no," Duncan said. "But remember the...stuff?"

Jake shook his head. "Thanks anyway, but I never got into coke."

Duncan shrugged. "No time like the present."

"I've got the wife and the kids."

"You were going to drink a case of beer in front of them, coke isn't much different." He lowered his voice. "Besides, half a line and they'll never know. I know what family holidays are like. I see couples coming in here arguing all the time. Kids yelling, parents yelling. Everyone's miserable. This'll take the edge off it and everyone will have a great time. If you ask me, it'd be irresponsible *not* to take a quick snort."

Duncan winked, and Jake couldn't help but smile. He was actually starting to like Duncan's admittedly bizarre take on life.

"And you're sure they'll never know?" Jake asked.

"Of course."

"Because if my wife even suspects..."

Duncan nodded. "Hell hath no fury?"

The two men nodded in shared understanding.

"I'll join you," Duncan said.

At the reception desk, Duncan lifted the bear statue and retrieved a bag. He tapped some powder onto the desk and made a couple of lines with the edge of a pamphlet.

Duncan started humming. "What's the name of that Christmas Carol? Let It Snow?"

Jake laughed. "I'm not sure if that's what they had in mind."

Duncan bent over the desk, but Jake interrupted him.

"Shouldn't we do it back in your office? What if someone walks in?"

Duncan shook his head.

"No one else is booked in tonight. We'll be fine." He slipped a drinking straw into his nose, then took a deep snort. He tipped his head back and rubbed his nostril, then grinned.

"And that's the way it's done," Duncan said. "It's got a bit of a tingle."

Jake looked through the glass doors. His vehicle was the only one there. Katherine and the kids were nowhere to be seen. But even so...

"I don't know if I should," Jake said.

"Come on, don't wuss out on me now," Duncan said. "Where's your Christmas spirit?"

Jake grunted, but he still smiled.

"Okay, okay. Just a bit."

He took the straw, closed his eyes, and breathed in. His body convulsed, not sure if it should cough or sneeze. He looked up at Duncan as he rubbed at his nose. Duncan was grinning and held his hand up for a high-five. Jake ignored it, and instead bent double and coughed.

Duncan slapped him on the back.

"Not bad, virgin."

Jake's eyes were watering, and his head felt light.

"Thanks, I guess. How long does it take this stuff to hit?"

"Not long. How you feeling?"

Jake shrugged. "My nose is a bit numb."

"It's cut with something else."

Jake looked at him, his grin suddenly gone.

"What do you mean something else? Cut with what?"

Duncan shrugged. "Don't know, I found this in a guest's room after they left. Could be anything really. But if you start seeing shit, don't be surprised."

Jake grabbed him by the collar and dragged him close. He could smell Duncan's sour breath.

"You told me it was safe, you little prick."

Duncan started at him wide-eyed. A smile twitched at the edge of his lip. And suddenly they were both laughing.

"Stop fucking laughing," Jake said, his own shoulders heaving as he laughed. He patted Duncan on the back.

Their laugher finally faded.

“Better get back to the family,” Jake said.

Duncan nodded. “Don’t forget your Esky.”

“Hey that reminds me, Katherine said our air conditioning is rooted.”

Duncan shrugged. “That’s funny, it was working before. I’ll come down and take a look.”

“You don’t need to.”

“Anything for our guests,” Duncan said and winked.

The heat and humidity seemed to suck the air right out of Jake’s lungs. Insects buzzed in the bush, and Jake waved away the flies that seemed to want to feast on his sweat. An extra big one tickled his skin and he slapped it. It caught between the cracks in his fingers. He dropped the Esky he’d been carrying one handed and examined the fly. It had such freakish eyes. And fine hairs over its body. It buzzed, but he held it firmly.

“You’re an ugly little bastard,” Jake whispered.

The fly seemed to turn its head.

Is that even possible?

It looked straight at him and grinned. Its teeth were sharp daggers. Hundreds of them.

“Who you calling ugly?” the fly asked.

Jake let out a yelp and threw it on the ground. It buzzed angrily, righted itself, and flew away.

“The little bastard talked.”

Duncan nodded. “Yep. They do that sometimes.”

Jake looked at him, his eyes wide with a combination of wonder and fear.

Duncan laughed loudly, tears springing from his eyes.

“Just kidding buddy,” he said between gasps of laughter. “Flies don’t talk you knob. You’re wasted.”

Jake laughed uneasily, the hundreds of razor sharp teeth still very real in his mind.

“I guess the coke hit in,” he said. “Just don’t tell my wife, okay?”

“Bros before hoes,” Duncan replied.

“What does that even mean?” Jake mumbled to himself as they made their way toward the cabin.

At the cabin, Katherine greeted them with a smile.

“Oh hi, Duncan,” she said. “You didn’t have to come all the way down here.”

“Couldn’t leave my favourite customers in the heat,” he said and stepped inside.

Jake followed him in. He was feeling a little lightheaded.

“You okay honey?” Katherine asked. “You look a little...off.”

Jake nodded. “Yeah, I’m okay. It’s the heat I guess. I don’t do well in heat and humidity.”

“Maybe you should sit down.”

“Yeah, take a load off,” Duncan said. “I’ll have this baby fixed up in no time.”

Duncan winked again at him.

What’s with all the damn winking?

Jake dropped into a wide, comfortable looking lounge. It didn’t disappoint. As soon as he settled he could feel his body relax. The voices in the room faded. Even the heat started to feel comforting. And he slept.

***

Jake jolted awake, the image of the fly still fresh in his mind. Its giant, all-seeing eyes. Its spindly legs and feet. And those teeth: hundreds of sharp needles sinking into his neck, tearing away at his flesh.

His heart was pounding and he squinted against the light. He noticed the colour had changed to a deeper orange. Just how long had he slept?

He wiped the sweat from the back of his neck and it came away sticky. He looked at his hand and screamed.

Blood.

He jumped from the chair and felt for the wound where the fly had sunk its teeth in, but his skin was smooth. No wound.

He ran to the kitchen and blasted the tap. The water was warm from the sun-beaten pipes, but he didn’t care. He scooped a handful onto his neck and rubbed the blood away. He just wanted it gone. No blood, no questions.

But the questions still remained. He turned the tap off and looked around the room. He realised the air conditioning was now humming peacefully, pouring cool air into the room. He even shivered a little.

He ran into the bedrooms. The bathroom. All empty. Where was Katherine? And the kids?

He ran back to the front door and slid it open.

"Katherine," he yelled.

He heard a rustling and ran to the steps. He saw Duncan disappearing into the bushes, his body rocking to the side as he lurched away.

"Duncan!"

Duncan turned, holding up a bloody knife, and gave Jake the finger. He grinned, and disappeared up the track toward reception.

Duncan could wait. Jake had to find his family. He tried not to think about the bloody knife.

He called out to his family again but he heard nothing. The sounds of the insects had once again closed in, making it hard to hear anything outside a ten metre radius.

On the floor of the forest he saw the marks, and his pulse quickened. The leaves had been scattered, the dried tops turned over to reveal the rotting vegetation below. That had to be Katherine and the kids.

"I'm coming honey!" he yelled, and vaulted over the railing, dropping to the forest floor below. His legs buckled, and a stab of pain ran up his leg. He tried to ignore it as he hobbled through the forest, following the path of rotten leaves.

The tracks led through deep drifts of leaving, winding away from the cabin and deeper into the forest. The air was still. No relief from the blanket of humidity. He sucked air into his lungs, forced it out again, and then sucked another breath in.

He kept thinking about Duncan, holding the knife high like some kind of damn trophy. Images flashed through his mind; dark images that on one level scared him, but on another level set him free. Duncan would pay.

Jake stopped running and listened. Was Duncan circling around? Taking another stab at his family?

He giggled at the pun, and then forced himself to stop. He ran his fingers through his hair. That damned cocaine. He needed to think. He needed some fresh air to clear his head.

He looked around for movement, but there was none. In the distance he saw a large dark shape. Another cabin.

He started running again.

“Katherine,” he gasped. “I’m coming baby!”

The cabin was similar to their own, but the veranda was scattered with leaves and it looked unkempt. It hadn’t been swept in a long time, and moss had started to grow on the exterior walls. But the leaves were disturbed.

His family – it had to be.

He jogged toward the cabin, his leg aching, his lungs feeling aflame and drowned at the same time. But he had to keep going. Had to find his family.

Had to kill Duncan.

He forced the thought from his mind. It repulsed him, though perhaps not as much as he would have thought.

His feet were heavy on the wooden steps. He clobbered towards the door, grabbed the handle and pulled. It didn't budge.

"Katherine," he yelled. He could have sworn he heard a scuffle inside. He banged on the glass. "It's me, let me in!"

Nothing. Was Duncan already inside?

He looked around for a rock or something to bust the glass. There was nothing. But then he saw it, and actually smiled. An ornate light built in the style of a late 1800's lantern hung from the wall near the door. He grabbed it with two hands and yanked. It popped from the wall too easily, and Jake fell backwards. He held the light in his hands and giggled. A piece of rotten wood was still attached to the base of the lamp. The cabin must have been so rotted that he could have just kicked a hole through the wall. But he had the light already, so it'd be a shame not to put it to use.

He stood, held the light above his head, and then brought it down on the glass door. It shattered, and tiny diamond-like fragments scattered across the floorboards inside.

Jake stepped inside.

"Katherine?" he called out, though a little softer this time. He needed to hear movement if Duncan really was in the cabin. Any surprise could mean the end of not just him but his family. He needed to live, even if it was just long enough to protect his them.

He stepped over the glass, walking deeper into the cabin. The shards crunched under his shoes.

"Katherine?" he whispered.

No answer.

He wished he had some kind of weapon, but there was no time to go hunting for something usable. Every second counted.

Stepping as lightly as possible he approached the main bedroom door and pushed it open. It creaked, and out of it flowed a musty smell. This cabin hadn't been used for years.

He walked into the room and knelt. He looked under the bed. Empty.

There were a set of built-in wardrobes, and he approached them carefully, again wishing he had some kind of weapon. He slid open one of the doors. A knife shot out, burying itself into his belly and he groaned. His fingers grabbed for the blade. There was no blood. And no blade. He looked down. No wound. The wardrobe was still shut.

He blinked rapidly, and rubbed his eyes with his palms. Fucking cocaine. Or whatever else was mixed into it.

Again he reached out, and slid open the door. There was a dark shape in the corner, and four eyes looked out at him. A high pitched scream drilled into his skull.

"Michael. Sari. It's only daddy."

He climbed into the wardrobe and pulled the doors closed. He wrapped his arms around his kids and held them tight, clamping his palms over their mouths.

"Shhh," he whispered. "Duncan might still be around. It's just Daddy. I'm going to let you go, but I need you to keep quiet. Do you understand?"

They both nodded, their little eyes still wide with fright.

He took his hands from their mouths. Neither screamed, but they both sat there rigidly. He briefly wondered how hard this was going to affect them, and if it'd have lasting effects; a future full of alcohol and expensive therapy sessions.

"Where's mummy?" he asked. He didn't know why he was talking to them like they were four years old again, but it seemed to calm them. Or calm him. Maybe both.

They remained silent.

"Come on kids, this is important. Where is mummy?"

Sari finally spoke.

"Reception," she said. "She's going for help."

Shit. That's where Duncan was headed.

"Okay, stay here. Keep quiet, and don't come out for anyone. Do you understand me?"

They both quickly nodded, and they somehow seemed to shrink even further into the corner, clinging to each other.

Jake left the wardrobe and slid the door closed behind him. He blinked away tears.

Katherine.

Duncan.

He ran from the cabin, the pain in his leg once again flaring up. He followed what was once a winding path leaving from the cabin back to what he hoped was reception. He thought it was the right direction, but it was hard to tell. Everything was starting to look the same.

His lungs laboured, but still he kept running. He hoped and prayed Katherine was still alive. If Duncan snuck up on her, it'd be over before she even knew it.

He felt himself crying again, and he wiped the tears away as he ran.

Branches pulled at his shirt, scraped his skin. He shoved them aside and kept forcing his feet forward.

He swatted another branch aside and almost laughed in relief. Ahead of him was the reception building. So close now. He felt his heart racing and wondered if it was the coke still flowing through his bloodstream, or whether it was just the heat and the fear. Not that it mattered. As long as it kept beating.

He ran toward reception and pushed through the front doors. The cold air sent a chill through his body, and goose-bumps sprung up on his arms.

"Katherine," he yelled.

"She's gone."

Jake spun towards the voice. Duncan sat in the waiting area amidst tourist pamphlets, photo books, and overpriced stuffed animals. He leaned forward on his chair, and with the bloody knife he drew a line of cocaine down the table. He had no straw, and so instead snorted it directly from the table.

He coughed and rubbed at his nose.

"Yep," Duncan said. "I don't know what they cut this with, but it's some bad, bad shit."

Jake looked at the bloody knife. His eyes darted towards the blood splattered on Duncan's shirt.

"Where is she?" Jake yelled and ran forward. He grabbed Duncan and lifted him from the chair. Jake felt powerful. He held Duncan in the air, the man's feet dangling off the ground.

"Where is she?" Jake whispered.

"Gone," Duncan said.

"I'll kill you."

Duncan laughed, but it turned into a cough.

"You already have," he said and pulled open his bloody shirt.

Jake saw the wound in Duncan's chest. It was weeping blood, and as the man sucked in another breath, air bubbled from the cut.

Jake dropped him.

Duncan fell back to his chair, and Jake slid into the one across the table.

He stared into the distance, not seeing anything. Not feeling anything. Just listening to the wheeze of Duncan's breathing.

An engine started and he looked behind him. He watched as his own car lurched backwards, paused, and then rocketed down the driveway, stones flicking up behind it.

"Your wife is one crazy-arse driver," Duncan said. His voice was weakening. "But I guess that's to be expected. You know, considering her husband is a crazy-arse killer."

"It's not true. It can't be," Jake said, but without conviction. It was true. He knew it. He felt it. He wished this all was a hallucination, but he could feel the truth. And the truth crushed him.

Tears again rolled down his cheeks, but these were tears of shame.

He nodded toward the cocaine scattered on the table. Duncan made a help-yourself gesture.

Taking the bloody knife, Jake carved a line, leaned forward, and sniffed deeply.

The second time round was easier. He rubbed his nose. He could feel the numbness return.

“Is Katherine alright?” he finally asked.

Duncan nodded. “You passed out in the chair. After I finished with your air-con I tapped you on the shoulder. You woke up and went bat-shit. Can’t hold your coke. Pussy.”

Jake nodded.

“Then what?” he asked.

Duncan shrugged. “Not much to tell. You ran around screaming like a lunatic. Something about a bee or something.”

“A fly,” Jake interrupted. “With teeth.”

Duncan nodded. He was weakening fast.

“Keep talking,” Jake said. “Please. I need to know.”

“Not much else to tell, my friend. You ran around screaming like a hysterical school girl. Grabbed a knife and stabbed me. You left the blade hanging out of me. So I took it and ran. Katherine and the kids ran. You collapsed back into your chair. I got twenty metres from the cabin when I heard you screaming after me, so I kept running. And here I am.”

“So Katherine is okay?”

“Physically, yeah. But you fucked with her mind. That broad will never sleep again.”

Jake lurched forward, grabbed the knife and held it against Duncan’s throat.

“She’s not a broad. She’s my wife.”

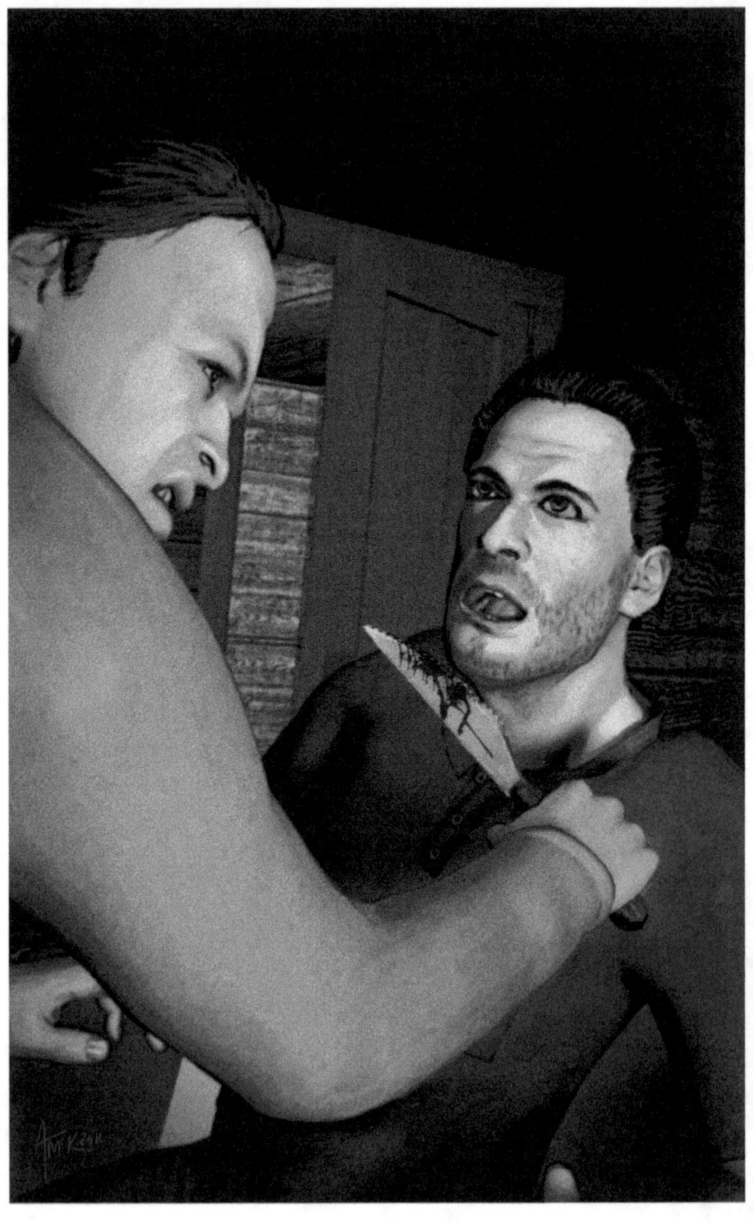

"Some way to treat your wife," Duncan croaked.

And then there was silence as the blood flowed. The air-conditioner hummed away and, outside, the insects buzzed.

***

Jake sat in his cabin, alone. He snorted another line of cocaine mixed with God-knows-what, and sat back in his lounge. The Christmas tree stood in front of him, and he admired it.

The tree was tastefully decorated. A few baubles, a few lengths of tinsel, some flashing lights, and the crowning glory: At the top of the tree was mounted Duncan's head.

"All I wanted was a beer," Jake told the head.

Duncan's dead eyes stared back. Gore dripped from the torn neck-hole, beading on the plastic branches of the Christmas tree.

A fly buzzed through the room and landed on Jake's leg. It turned its head and looked at him.

"You're one messed up motherfucker," it said. With a hiss it bared its teeth; hundreds of razor sharp needles.

Jake slapped it with his palm, picked up the stunned fly, dropped it into his mouth and chewed.

"Your teeth are no match for mine," he said.

He leaned forward, took another snort of cocaine, sat back and started to hum. The lights of the tree flashed on and off, and he softly sung.

“Let it snow, let it snow, let it snow...”

UNWANTED GIFT

BELINDA DORIO

I woke alone, as I often did now on Christmas morning. There were no flashing lights on my non-existent Christmas tree, no stockings on hanging from the mantle and there was definitely no pitter-patter of children's feet as they ran around excitedly. It was silent apart from the grandfather clock ticking loudly from the lounge, worsening my mood. I don't know why I hadn't gotten rid of the old thing.

My new friends once joked that I was the Grinch, but they didn't understand my distaste for Christmas and they never would. I'd made sure of that. I patted my coffee maker absently. "Merry Christmas," I said to it as it sparkled back at me.

It wasn't until I was curled up comfortably on the couch with my steaming cup of black coffee that I noticed the box on top of the TV. My heart stilled in my chest. It was shiny and red and had annoying, cheery reindeers prancing all over it. My grip on the mug tightened and I imagined it shattering everywhere from the pressure. It wouldn't do that. I was too weak. I placed my mug down and tried to pretend that my hands weren't shaking. *Pull yourself together Megan.* I straightened and took a deep breath. My hands were clammy as I brushed the front of my pajamas. I eased my slippers off silently and padded bare-foot to the front door, straining my ears for any noise – but all I could hear was that damn clock. *Tick, tock, tick.* My fingers found the cool steel of the dead-bolt on the door. Locked. Relief flooded through me in an icy wash that made my fingertips tingle.

I turned slowly back to the present on top of the TV, sitting so innocently. Maybe I was over-reacting; one of the girls could have somehow left it for me as a joke. They knew I hated presents. Of course. That's what it was. Just some silly joke. *It's just a prank, Megan.* I took another deep breath, this one not as shaky. I walked back to the TV and took the gift in my hands. I lifted the lid and peered inside, but there was nothing but a single piece of folded paper. I tried to swallow past a lump in my throat as I felt sweat drip down my neck. *It's hot in here.* The small scraping noise of the paper being lifted from the box seemed loud in the silent house, with the grandfather clock still ticking. My eyes read the words on the paper, but my brain refused to see the meaning and I had to re-read it a few times before a chill crept over my skin. *Run Megan, run.* But I couldn't. I was riveted to the spot. Panic clamped around my heart with its icy grip. Wasn't there supposed to be a fight or flight instinct? I wondered when it would kick in.

He spoke then, from somewhere behind me. And his voice was like a nightmare come to life, like if you were a child and discovered there really was a bogey man in your closet. I didn't hear what he said, but I knew it was him. Tears pricked at my eyes as fear lay heavy in my gut. My hand clenched and his words crumpled with the paper.

Merry Christmas, - it had said- **I've missed you.**

He sat casually in one of my armchairs and his legs dangled off the side. Sunlight danced across his clear blue eyes and I shuddered as he smiled a lop-sided smile at me. I knew that smile all too well. It said 'See, I'm harmless' but I knew Clay was anything but. Clay and I had dated once. He had been my first love. We met through mutual friends, many years ago now. But I could still picture the way Kelly's eyes pleaded with me when she pulled me aside to warn me about him. If only I'd listened.

"I know he seems sweet and that he is totally cute" she'd breathed in a whispered voice, her hand gripping my arm tightly as her eyes darted back to the bar table where the boys had sat. "But he's bad news, Megs. Please trust me on this." But Kelly always was a worry wart. She was overly paranoid about everything from burglars to what additives were in her food. Kelly had been with her boyfriend Jason for years, and jealousy had always burned at me when I saw them together. It seemed like I was always alone and unwanted. Clay was one of Jason's closest friends, and Jason was nice enough. So how bad could Clay be? I'd thought that maybe Kelly just didn't want me to be happy. I had loved the way Clay's eyes followed me around the bar, watching my every move with his bright blue eyes as I put an extra swing into my step – teasing him. Our first kiss hadn't been the romantic encounter I'd expected, but was rough, his teeth biting at my bottom lip as his mouth crushed down on mine. In hindsight, it was a warning I had failed to pick up on.

The relationship had started out as all relationships do – well. He took me away often and when we went out together I loved the way he was so protective of me. I felt safe with Clay. After just a year he had gotten down on one knee and produced a diamond ring, and I'd said yes, but Kelly continued to warn me – she didn't understand our love. Clay encouraged me to stop talking to her, and I obeyed. As he had slid the engagement ring on to my finger a strange look came into his eyes and he kissed my forehead before whispering "mine".

It wasn't until we moved in together that the warning bells started to ring. Being around Clay twenty-four-seven allowed me to see all of him, and I learnt that my sweetheart had an ugly temper. We would argue and he would yell and scream at me if I was home late from work, demanding to know where I had been. His blue eyes would shine with rage in a way I had never seen. If I tried to escape his temper by leaving the house he became enraged further, so I learnt to come home early and to not yell back. I hated to see his hands clenching and unclenching as he yelled, but Clay would never hurt me- would he?

Clay didn't like me going out without him, so I began to neglect my girlfriends and eventually they stopped bothering to ask me out with them. I'd felt like I was being a terrible fiancé, so I tried to make it work. I tried to do everything Clay wanted from me.

I had not once in our relationship denied Clay sex when he wanted it. But one day I had come home from work feeling especially drained and over-tired. When I told him I was too tired, he continued to fondle me. His hand reached down under my panties and I had grabbed it before it got any lower.

"Clay, I said *no*," I ground out through my teeth and I'd felt him still beside me. I thought for a moment he would apologise and let me sleep, but I couldn't see the rage build in his eyes with the lights out. That night my fiancé of nearly two years raped and beat me, staying silent the whole time - even when I begged him to stop.

My mother had taken me to the police station where I pressed charges. Clay was jailed for a year, and a restraining order restricted him from contacting me in any way when he was released. But I still hadn't felt safe. I moved from the city centre of Sydney and traded the hustle and bustle of city life for outback silence in a remote part of Western Australia. I hadn't even kept track of the dates, so I didn't know how long he had been released for.

"How did you find me?" Thankfully my voice didn't shake like my hands.

He shrugged slightly, the lop-sided grin still on his face. "I've been here awhile, sweetie. Watching you. Making sure you weren't being a naughty girl while I was gone." His voice had a sing-song quality about it.

"I have a restraining order against you. You can't be here."

He frowned.

"You're not being very nice, sweetie. I've waited very patiently to talk to you. I wanted to surprise you for Christmas. I know how much you like surprises" his eyes danced with icy humour. My stomach roiled. It had been Christmas Eve when Clay attacked me. I stared at him. The light that was in his eyes when I met him was now wiped clean, leaving his blue eyes cold and merciless. How could he have turned so cruel? I took a step back and bumped the television, and a small yelp escaped my lips.

Clay sat still, the humour drained out of his face. His relaxed posture looked stiff, like a wolf waiting to pounce.

"What do you want?" I asked breathlessly, and hated myself for the fear I could hear in my voice.

"What I always wanted. You." He lunged for me.

I ran. My heart pounded blood in my ears as my bare feet slapped hard against the tiles of the kitchen. I could hear him behind me, not far away. I didn't dare turn around. A childhood memory floated through my mind of a teacher asking the class what we should do if we thought there was a stranger in the house. 'Call the police' one child answered, and 'hide' said another. The teacher shook her head and replied sternly; 'No, children. You get out!' *Back door Megan. Go for the backdoor.*

The laundry loomed into view and my heart gave a flit of hope. My breathing was coming hard and my hands shook violently as I tried to unlock the laundry door that led into the garden. But then hands clamped around my waist and lifted me from the door. *Too slow Megan. You're too slow. Too weak.* I shrieked louder than I thought possible and kicked my legs out as my fingers tried to grip the door frame, but my face was wet from the tears streaming down my face. *Red. Red.* Everything seemed to have a red backwash as I screamed over and over again. Clay's strong arms pulled me free from the door. I struggled, but he was stronger and he pinned my arms before pressing me to the cold floor of the laundry. I saw him swing his arm back and my mind shorted out for a moment. *Pain. Pain.*

"Shut up, sweetie," Clay said through clenched teeth, still holding my writhing body in place. My screaming subsided and a pathetic whimper escaped. My head began to throb and the side of my face stung all too familiarly. *Let him kill me. Don't let him touch me.* But Clay had other ideas. In one swift movement he ripped the front of my singlet open, leaving my chest bare, and he stared for a moment before his calloused hands began to fondle me.

"God, I've missed you sweetie. God!" His hands were rough as he pulled and tugged at me causing more pathetic whimpers to fall from my mouth. I could hear something else as well, speaking over and over again. I realised with a start it was my voice.

"Please don't," I was saying, over and over again. He seemed to have enough of seeing my tear streaked face so he flipped me over and my hips ground hard into the cold tile floor, as another scream escaped. I felt a burst of adrenaline and I tried to crawl for the door. My hands desperately slapped the ground. My knees scraped on the tiles. But one firm tug from those strong hands and I was back on my belly, screaming my frustration.

"Leave me alone!" I shouted. I felt his hands tugging at my pants and my stomach turned. I was going to be sick.

A noise came that my mind couldn't decipher and Clay's hands on my hips stilled. The sound revealed itself as a knock at the front door, louder the second time. I drew in a breath to scream again but Clay's rough hand fell over my mouth, before I could let it out. *Help me! I'm in here!* I screamed in my head as Clay bent and whispered in my ear.

"Shhhhh.... we wouldn't want anyone to come and ruin our fun, would we?" My stomach flipped again and I closed my eyes as I willed myself not to throw up. I heard a man's voice.

"Megan?" *Ted! Oh, thank God. It was Ted!*

Ted was a burly retired police officer who lived next door, but out here next door was still pretty far away. I thanked my lucky stars that today was Christmas. Ted must have come over to check on me – as he often did. I presumed he felt sorry for me but I couldn't deny that I enjoyed the company of the older man and his fatherly presence. He was one of the only people in this small town who knew my story; the only one I had confided in.

Clay's hand over my mouth squeezed painfully tight.

"Now sweetie, who is that?" My heart thudded in my chest as I waited for what I knew was coming. That ugly, ugly jealousy that loomed over Clay like a dark cloud. He grabbed my hair and I winced. "I always knew you were a slut, cheating on me and lying to me." His hand shook where it was knotted in my hair. He was so devoured by rage that he did not see Ted come to the back window, Clay did not see Ted's eyes widen as they met mine before he shot out of sight again. I hoped Ted had his gun with him. I had to do something. *Think Megan, think.*

Clay was pulling my hair tighter, and his hand that covered my mouth moved to squeeze my nostrils closed . A fresh wave of panic washed over me. *This is it.* The love of my life was going to kill me. My mind screamed at me to move, to flail and to kick as my brain was deprived oxygen. But instead I waited a moment and went slack in his arms, hoping he would think I had lost consciousness. It worked. He dropped me to the ground and I inhaled a gulp of air as quietly as I could. I could hear him fumbling for his belt buckle and I lay as still as I could. He leant over me, hands on my hips again, and I kicked both my legs up with all my strength. He screamed out, clutching his vulnerable and naked parts, and I sprung up and ran for the door. He was too slow this time and the lock came undone easily under my hands. Only a second had passed before Ted burst through the door- gun raised. But Clay had recovered and knocked the older man to the ground. The black handgun slid along the ground and came to a stop at my toes. I looked at it, then back to the struggling men on my laundry floor where blood was splattered here and there. As if in a dream, I bent and my hands found the cold steel of the gun. It was heavy and cumbersome in my small hands. But they didn't shake as I raised the gun to the two men tangled amongst each other.

"Clay!" I shouted and he looked up at me. Blood covered his hands and his face where he had beaten and been beaten. Seeing his face bloodied gave my heart a happy flip and my hands were steady as they held the gun.

As Clay's hands began to strangle the life out of poor old Ted, he smiled up at me with that lop-sided grin that I'd fallen in love with.

"You couldn't shoot me sweetie. You love me."

"I *loved* you," I whispered before I gave the trigger the slightest squeeze.

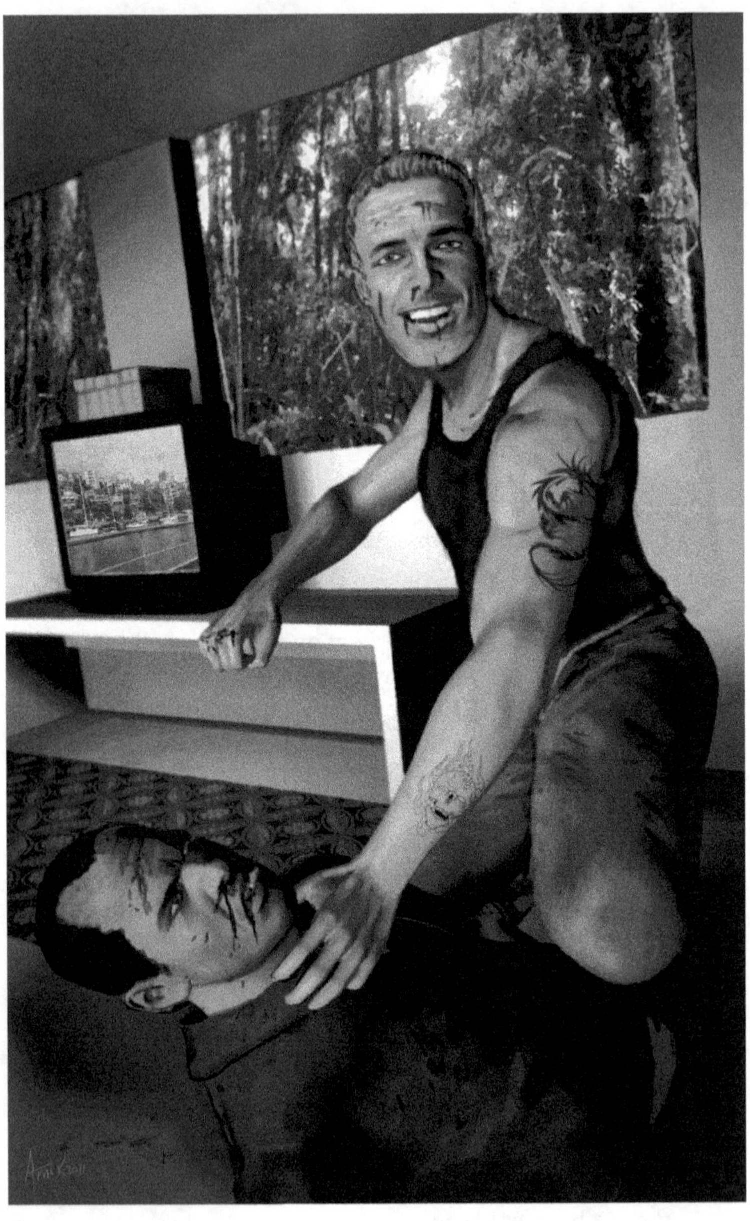

One, two. The gunshots were deafening to my ears as blood blossomed on Clays white shirt where he lay crumpled on the floor. His hand moved down to touch his wound before he looked at his bloody hand, then back to me, then back to his hand. The light slowly faded from his eyes and his last breath rattled from his lips. Ted scrambled up. I think he was saying something but there was a ringing in my ears that didn't seem to want to go away. The old police officer collected the gun. I hadn't even noticed I'd dropped it. I tried to hold my singlet closed. He looked up at me and said something again before shaking his head. A look like sadness creapt into his eyes as his eyebrows knitted together in a frown. He placed a hand on my shoulder and led me out the back door where he sat me on the back step. I guess he went back in to see if my Clay had a pulse. I knew he wouldn't. I had watched the light in his eyes splutter out as his life bled out from the bullet holes in his chest. My stomach turned again and this time it won the fight as my vomit splattered the grass.

The police came soon after, how soon I wasn't sure. Time seemed to be seeping away from me and only the *tick, tock* of my old grandfather clock in the lounge reminded me of its passing. Some nice police officers had shown me where Clay had been living for the last month, in my roof. I had never known that people could get inside your house by simply moving a few roof tiles and making a hole. He had slipped in and waited, watching me from the vent in the bathroom and the heating ducts in my bedroom.

"What was he waiting for?" Asked a high female voice that belonged to a young police officer whose uniform looked too clean and too ironed. A newbie.

"Christmas," I said, my voice sounding far away. "He was waiting for Christmas."

NAUGHTY OR NICE

CAMERON TROST

'How many times do I have to tell you not to play with scissors, Barry? Don't forget, Father Christmas doesn't leave presents for children who don't behave themselves.'

'What?!' Barry looked at his father as though he had gone mad. It was probably the most ridiculous thing he had ever heard. 'That's not true, dad. All kids get presents at Christmas. *All* kids do – *every* year.'

Kevin shook his head adamantly. Barry was stunned as his childish mind tried to comprehend the unpleasant truth.

'No, they certainly do not. If you misbehave too much then Father Christmas will give your present to another little boy somewhere in the world – one who knows how to be good. That's how it has always been and that's how it will always be. Haven't they taught you that carol at school, the one where it says, *He's making a list, checking it twice, gonna find out who's naughty or nice, Santa Claus is comin' to town...?*'

Barry decided to stop cutting locks of long, blonde hair off his big sister's favourite doll for a second. But it was already too late; the once glamorous plastic model now looked more like a B-grade horror movie prop. He was contemplating what his dad had told him and trying to remember the words to the carol that would support his dad's argument. Then, after a few long seconds of deep thought, he looked up at his father and frowned. He had come to a decision.

'That's bullshit!'

Kevin was taken aback.

'Barry! I'll wash your mouth out with soap, young man. Don't use words like that!'

'*You* say that word, dad.'

Kevin winced. He hated it when he noticed his own shortcomings in his children but he was definitely not going to let Barry use that as an excuse. 'Yes, well... I'm not seven years old! When you're my age you can speak however you like.'

Barry just looked at his father blankly, unable to comprehend why he should have to follow a different set of rules simply because he was a child.

Kevin took the scissors from his son's hand, being careful not to cut himself, and looked at the mangled doll.

'You've ruined your sister's doll. She'll be angry. I'm sure you won't be getting any presents this Christmas.'

Barry scowled and tossed the disfigured doll aside as though it were just a piece of rubbish. It landed between the magazine rack and the couch and lay there like the unlucky victim of a tiny man-eating monster. The thought of not receiving presents for Christmas was unimaginable. He had received at least one or two every year since he was a baby and this year he was expecting a big one. He had been waiting anxiously for a new bicycle ever since he rode his old one off an embankment near the railway station and twisted its frame when it landed on the concrete path below.

'I haven't been naughty this year.'

Kevin fought the urge to laugh at his son's blatant lie. This was a serious talk they were having and he had to show Barry that he was not at all satisfied with his mischievous behaviour. Being naughty was one thing but denying the fact was another altogether. Kevin did not want his boy to grow up thinking that dishonesty was acceptable – he might end up becoming a criminal – or worse still, a politician.

'*You* haven't been naughty?'

'Nope,' he said sulkily, sticking his bottom lip out.

'You have a long, long list of naughty acts, Barry. I don't know where to begin. Let me think... wait a minute... yes, I do. What about Bobby?'

'What?'

'You don't remember?'

Barry shrugged his shoulders and allowed a blank expression to cover his face in a shameless attempt to pretend that he had no recollection of the incident.

'You broke his leg with a cricket bat. Do you understand what that means, to *break* somebody's leg?'

Barry rolled his eyes and let out a sigh. 'Yeah, it means to make it hurt.'

'That's right,' Kevin nodded. 'That was very naughty, wasn't it?'

'I guess,' the boy admitted, pretending to feel sorry but not succeeding in convincing Kevin that he regretted the incident one bit.

'That's not all. There are plenty of other very bad things that you have done this year. How about your class excursion to the Lone Pine Koala Sanctuary? Does that ring a bell?'

'Ring a bell?'

'Yeah, that means, *do you remember what happened?*'

'I hurted some animals.'

'That's right, you *hurt* some animals. You even jumped on one and killed it. A poor little joey. Do you understand that? To kill something?'

'It means you make it be dead,' Barry explained.

'That's right. You shouldn't kill animals, Barry – ever.' Kevin hesitated for an instant. 'Unless maybe you eat them afterwards, then I suppose it's all right.

Although, vegetarians believe that... anyway, that's not the point. You just shouldn't hurt or kill anything.'

'Miss Moffatt says that all living things have a white to life.'

'That's right, Barry. They have a *right* to life. Maybe you should listen to her more carefully. She's a smart teacher.' *And what a cute little arse she has too!* Kevin thought to himself.

'If I say I'm sorry, will Father Christmas leave me a present? I really want a new bike.' Barry made a sad face. 'I miss my old one.'

Kevin smiled at his son sympathetically.

'Perhaps – I tell you what, if you only do good things between now and Christmas you will be sure to get a present. If you can do that, I will send Father Christmas a letter myself to let him know that you have made a real effort to change. By showing him – and me – that you are serious about being a good boy, he might decide to forgive you.'

Barry was silent for a moment, looking at the floor. His seven year old brain seemed to be deep in contemplation. He was weighing up his options. The choice was simple, be good for a couple of weeks or risk not getting a new bicycle.

'I'll be good from now until Christmas.'

'Do you promise?'

He nodded his head in agreement.

Kevin did not believe him for a minute but pretended that he had faith in his son's ability to keep his word. The promise was a very ambitious one; Christmas was still two weeks away. Two weeks of being a good boy would be difficult for Barry - but he would try.

*　　　*　　　*

The fortnight passed by and Barry, much to his parents' surprise, managed to avoid getting up to anything particularly naughty. He even apologised humbly to his big sister when she discovered the twisted remains of her favourite doll.

On Christmas Eve, after a delightful night of singing along with the Carols by Candlelight broadcast and eating as much as they wanted, Barry and his sister were put to bed by their mother. Once she had reminded them that Father Christmas would not leave them any presents if they did not go to sleep straight away, she turned all the upstairs lights off and went down to the master bedroom. She closed and locked the door behind her.

'The kids are definitely asleep?' Kevin, who in her absence had dressed himself up as Father Christmas, asked urgently through his bushy white beard.

She repressed a laugh at finding the legendary bringer of presents lying where her husband should have been – but the last minute change in partner did not seem to bother her. She took her dressing gown off and exposed her curvy body.

'Yes, I tucked them in and told them that if they got out of bed before the sun came up then they wouldn't get any presents.'

'Ho, ho, ho... very good - that means we've got all night.'

‘That’s right,’ Danielle whispered as Bing Crosby softly crooned White Christmas in the background. She blew him a kiss. Then her right hand disappeared behind her back and her red bra with fluffy white trimming dropped gracefully onto the bed. Kevin nodded his head in appreciation as a familiar pair of round breasts was exposed. They reminded him of the delicious desert they had eaten earlier that evening; custard covered plum pudding topped with a cherry.

‘I love Christmas,’ she whispered with bright red lips to the white-bearded man kneeling beside her on the bed.

‘Ho-ho-ho, me too!’ Kevin replied.

She reached into his red coat and pulled out the pillow he had used for a belly.

‘That’s better,’ she smiled naughtily, ‘I can handle the beard – that’s kind of sexy – but not the belly.’

Her boobs were alpine peaks waiting to be conquered by a courageous explorer. She rubbed them against the bearded face.

‘So where do you want to start, Father Christmas?’ She asked, making her chest jiggle. ‘With dancer... or prancer?’

‘Tough choice... let’s start with dancer!’ He lunged forward and smothered “dancer” with his snow white beard. His lips closed in on the nipple. Father Christmas was going to have a very busy night indeed.

* * *

Barry woke up in the middle of the night because he had to do wee-wee. He had not forgotten what his mum had told him, that if he got out of bed before dawn Father Christmas would not leave him any presents, but he did not really have a choice. He was busting to go to the toilet.

The little boy pushed his covers back and slipped out of bed. It was a silent night and the three other members of the household were presumably all fast asleep. Barry stepped over to the bedroom door and carefully opened it. He entered the hallway and crept through the heavy darkness that pervaded the house, trying not to make the floorboards creak. He advanced on his tippy-toes, like a burglar, as he slowly made his way along the hallway where an invisible clock was ticking the seconds away. He had still not worked out how Father Christmas managed to get into houses in sunny Queensland, where chimneys were rare, but that did not really matter. What was important was that he did not come across the jolly old man by accident. It had not been easy to behave himself for two whole weeks and the last thing he wanted was to ruin all that now and miss out on getting a new bicycle.

Barry moved stealthily through the kitchen and into the bathroom. He had to do wee-wee as quietly as he could and did not even turn the light on because he was afraid that it might draw attention. He did not care if he urinated on the toilet seat or even on the floor, just so long as Father Christmas did not catch him and deprive him of his new bike. At any rate, some light from the street lamps and crescent moon outside was shining softly through the bathroom window. It provided just enough light for Barry to distinguish between the white ring of the toilet seat and the slightly darker area which seemed to be the water at the bottom of the bowl.

As Barry urinated, he stopped now and then to listen to the silence, checking that nothing disturbed it. The house was as quiet as the grave. He couldn't even hear his father's snoring or the ticking of the hallway clock. When he resumed, Barry used the change in sound between sharp ceramic chime and dull plastic splash to help him decide how to alter the trajectory of the flow. He felt some urine drip onto his bare feet but wasn't too concerned – just so long as Father Christmas didn't catch him.

Everything was going well until Barry had finished relieving himself and was about the sneak back to his bed. The silence that reigned within the house was disrupted by the sound of creaking floorboards. At first, it was difficult to tell whether somebody was moving around or it was just the natural creaking of wood. Barry peered through the obscurity to the feint outline of the bathroom doorway but he could not see anybody moving through the darkness, just the usual shadowplay on the walls caused by moonlight shining through windows and the branches of the palm trees in the backyard.

Then the creaking grew louder and a dark shape appeared. Barry wanted to think that he was just imagining it all, but as the shape drew closer it became more substantial. Its form was easier to distinguish with every step. Although Barry could not see who it was, he could tell that the shape was a big, round one. The possibility that it was Father Christmas was very high and Barry did not want to risk being caught out of bed by him. He had to think and act very quickly but it was already too late for him to slip out of the bathroom without being noticed. He had to find somewhere to hide inside the bathroom. But just where could he hide? His young mind raced frantically. Of course! The shower was his best refuge. If he hid behind the shower curtain he just might get away with being out of bed. Father Christmas probably needed to do wee-wee or, at worst, a poo. He was certainly not planning on taking a shower. Barry made his move.

A few seconds later, Father Christmas arrived in the bathroom and switched the light on. Barry was already crouched down behind the floral shower curtain, breathing as softly as he could and making every effort not to move at all. The sudden burst of light was harsh and made Barry shut his eyes for a moment, but then he let them ease warily open again.

The blurry red shape on the other side of the plastic curtain looked like a giant tomato. It stopped in front of the toilet and released a loud, annoyed sigh. Barry kept his mouth firmly closed to prevent himself from being tempted to say something in his defence. He knew exactly why Father Christmas had sighed.

'Barry...' Father Christmas said to himself, and started unrolling a length of toilet paper. 'What a bloody mess he has made! I thought I had taught him to aim before he shoots!'

The boy forced himself not to react and give himself away. He had no idea what the usually jolly man meant about teaching him to aim. Only his father had ever tried to teach him how to aim properly when taking a leak.

Barry just kept breathing softly and hoped that the bearded man would not take too long to wipe up and then empty his bladder. He crossed his fingers, hoping that his poor toilet technique would not cost him his new bicycle.

Father Christmas unrolled some toilet paper and wiped the seat clean before urinating. It seemed to take him an eternity. He was just about to finish up and leave the bathroom when he turned and seemed to look straight at the shower curtain. He had detected that there was something out of place behind it.

Barry held his breath and tightened every muscle in his body. He wished he had stayed in bed after all, despite his need to take a leak. He had done his best to behave himself for two long weeks and now all of that was about to be ruined just because he had needed to go to the loo. It wasn't fair. It wasn't his fault that he needed to do wee-wee. He still deserved to get a new bicycle.

'What's that?' Father Christmas said to himself through his big white beard, a mix of curiosity and confusion hanging from his words. He took a step forward and reached out for the plastic shower curtain. Barry remained frozen. There was nowhere to go – he was cornered. The hand drew the shower curtain back and the white-bearded face frowned - but it also expressed relief.

'Barry? What's going on? Why in the world are you sitting in the shower?'

The little boy was stunned like a wild animal caught in the headlights of a road train. He was lost for words – until desperation forced him to say something in his defence.

'Santa... I'm sorry! I had to do wee-wee.'

Kevin smiled behind his white beard, glad that he had fallen asleep after his Christmas Eve love-making without taking the costume off. Barry did not recognise him - he really thought it was Santa Claus who had come to use the family bathroom. Children's imaginations were really incredible – what a shame that adulthood smothered them.

Kevin thanked his lucky stars that he had not come out naked because, while he was urinating, he had noticed that a red smudge covered much of his penis. If the boy had seen that and somehow made the connection between the colour on his father's private parts and the shade of lipstick his mother had been wearing earlier that night... well, that would have been very embarrassing for Kevin and earthshakingly confusing for Barry. However, he had not made that mistake. He was still dressed up as Santa Claus and his son had no idea that it was really his father. Kevin had to take advantage of the situation to have some fun. This was the ideal opportunity to get Barry to admit to his habit of getting up to mischief.

'Are you being a naughty boy, Barry?' He asked using an unnaturally deep voice.

'No, Father Christmas. I just needed to do wee-wee. I promise. I'm never naughty.'

'Is that so? Never ever? Are you sure?' His eyes bore into the boy's. 'You wouldn't lie to me, would you?'

'No, Sir,' the little boy confirmed, still crouching in the corner of the shower cubicle.

'What about when you broke little Bobby's leg with a cricket bat? That wasn't exactly nice of you, was it?'

Barry looked up at Father Christmas with an angelic face that portrayed an image of pure innocence and honesty. Kevin had been expecting a look of amazement on his son's face but it seemed that he was not surprised at all that Father Christmas knew all about him. Nevertheless, he was determined to deny any wrong-doing.

'Who's Bobby?' He asked.

'Your friend, Bobby... You broke his leg with a cricket bat.'

Barry shrugged his shoulders.

'Is that true, Barry?'

'I don't know any Bobby... and I never play cricket.'

Kevin's hidden smile turned into a disappointed frown. He knew that his son was naughty but he had no idea that he was capable of lying through his teeth to Father Christmas himself.

'What about the little kangaroo you killed at the koala sanctuary? That was very naughty too.'

Barry shook his head. 'You must think I'm another little boy.'

Father Christmas shook his head slowly. 'No, I'm talking about *you*, Barry.'

'Maybe you been talkin' to my dad, Father Christmas, but it's all lies. Sometimes he drinks too much beer and imagines things. I haven't never gone to the koala sanctuary. Daddy's full of shit!'

Father Christmas lost his cool – his cheeks turned as red as his clothes and his beard quivered angrily. He lurched forward like a possessed Egyptian mummy and reached out for Barry with his giant hands, but the boy sprang aside before he could get a hold of him. Barry was scared. He had seen Father Christmas before, in shopping centres and playgrounds – even at school, but he had never seen him lose his temper. Father Christmas was always a jolly fellow who loved being around children. Barry might have been very young but he was already old enough to know that people who always seemed to be good-tempered were the most dangerous on the rare occasions when they blew a fuse. He had to accept the fact that Father Christmas was capable of really hurting him.

Barry decided that he had to fight back – it was a matter of survival. As Father Christmas stepped into the shower cubicle, he snapped into action. He kicked at a red trousered leg and made it slip. Father Christmas lost his footing and fell heavily, almost crushing the boy under him but only landing on one of his legs. Barry yelled out. He had a sharp pain in his thigh and guessed that maybe it was broken, the way he had broken Bobby's leg. It sure did hurt.

All of a sudden a screaming sound pierced Barry's ears. He looked up and saw that it was his mum standing in the bathroom doorway. She was naked except for a tiny pair of red panties with furry trimming. Her red lipstick was smeared all over her mouth.

'My leg hurts, mummy. Father Christmas fell on it!'

But she was not listening to Barry. She could not care less about his leg. She was just screaming and shaking all over, her breasts jingling like the bells in Barry's favourite Christmas carol.

'What's happening?' It was Barry's sister – she had been woken up by all the commotion. Fear stained her voice.

'I needed to go to the toilet real bad,' Barry told his mum.

She was still ignoring him, her gaze fixed on the red shape lying in the shower cubicle. Its white beard was changing colour. It was starting to match the clothing. Red was taking hold – but not bright red – dark red.

Every now and then, when Danielle stopped screaming to catch her breath, another noise, much quieter but equally disturbing, filled Barry's ears.

It was the sound of liquid dripping down the shower drain.

Barry tried to crawl out from under the weight that was pinning his leg. He pushed at the red lump that trapped him with all the might his little arms could muster. At the same time, he wriggled his leg. It hurt a lot but he managed to free himself and crawl out of the shower.

He looked around. His mother and her screaming were no longer there at the doorway. He could not see where she had gone. She had rushed off somewhere, but he thought he could hear the electronic beeping of a telephone number being dialled. Then he heard his sister scream at his mother. Her voice sent a chill through the air. *'What has Barry done now?'*

Father Christmas was still not moving. His red bearded face lay motionless against the tiles of the shower cubicle.

The horrible dripping continued, even though the shower head and taps were not leaking.

Barry frowned as he looked at the red lump. He forced himself to accept the fact that the red liquid dripping into the drain was blood.

Father Christmas was dead, his skull cracked open by the fall.

Barry had made him angry with his lies and accidentally killed him. He was sure that this was the naughtiest thing he had ever done, even worse than breaking Bobby's leg or killing the cute little joey on his class excursion. He had destroyed Christmas – that was really bad.

Barry's throat choked up as a sense of regret overwhelmed his little body. If he had known that this was going to happen he would have done wee-wee in bed like he had when he was younger.

Drip... drip... drip.

He started crying uncontrollably, as he understood the terrible significance of what had just happened. Father Christmas was dead after so many hundreds of years. Dead for ever after, just like the joey. There was no coming back now. He was as dead as a doornail – dead before he had been able to deliver all his presents.

The horrible consequence of the situation made Barry feel sick inside, and he started crying. He shed tears, not for Father Christmas, but for the present he would not receive. There was no way he was getting his new bike now…

SATAN CLAUS

KEITH MUSHONGA

Dong! The final chime rang through the small church and into the town. The midnight mass burst into song and the faces of the revellers beamed like the sun at midday. Another Christmas had arrived.

Another sound, unheard by the singers and far more unusual, particularly for Christmas, happened out in the graveyard behind the church. The ground opened with a rip and a rumble. A gaping hole, two metres long, one metre wide and some three metres deep appeared. A few seconds later, an abomination emerged from the crevasse. A grey-skinned corpse in a soil-covered Father Christmas suit climbed out of the ground. Bugs crawled from its ears, nostrils and mouth, which was stuck in a hideous and mostly toothless grin. Its eyes were red and two small bones protruded from high on its forehead.

The demonic creature shook itself and sent bugs and soil flying. It looked at the church as the sound of the worshippers' song reached it. The maniacal grin widened and Satan Claus knew what it had to do.

*   *   *

A few streets away, on the outskirts of town, Leonie and Brad spoke in hushed voices as they prepared their children's presents beneath their brightly decorated Christmas tree. Their two youngest children, Davey and Jessica, were asleep in their beds, while their eldest child, Megan, was returning home from her boarding school in Melbourne early in the afternoon.

"It is such a shame that Megan didn't bus it here earlier," Leonie told her husband.

"I know. She'd rather be with those hooligan friends of hers in the city than with her family. She's changed so much over the last nine months or so. Poor little Jess is really feeling it."

"I hope she doesn't spoil Christmas."

"We are probably lucky and should be grateful that she is coming at all. She doesn't believe anymore, you know."

With a tear in her eye, Leonie picked up a small crucifix Davey had made at Sunday school and fastened it to the Christmas sock she had sewn for Megan. "She'll come around," she said hopefully. "I am sure she will."

*   *   *

"It is time to go to bed. No more drinks," the student rep called into the boarding school living room, at no one in particular.

Two teenage girls each picked up a third from the floor.

"I don't think so!" Megan retorted. "The night is still young."

"You have to be on a bus tomorrow morning and it won't be a fun trip if you're hung over," said Lauren.

"I wish I wasn't going."

A part of Megan really did feel that way. Another part was racked with guilt. This time last year, she had been at home, helping her parents with the presents. Now, she was about as drunk as she had ever been and an underage alcoholic. A part of Megan wanted to stay at the boarding school and drink herself to oblivion. Another part wanted her innocence and childhood back.

* * *

As Satan Claus approached the front door of the church, a car screeched into the gravel parking lot at high speed, spraying small stones everywhere. The car came to a skidding halt and a young couple jumped quickly from the car. They ran towards the church, giggling and poking each other along the way.

"I can't believe we both fell asleep," the man chortled.

"It must have been the alcohol."

"The pastor won't be happy with us." He winked knowingly.

"He ... ooh," she squeaked and pointed. "Father Christmas is here."

"Have you been rolling around in the dirt mate?" he asked the guy in the Santa suit.

There was no reply.

As the light from a lantern near the door to the church crossed the face of Satan Claus, the woman gasped. "Are you okay? You look hurt."

Its mad grin intensified and before either of the couple could scream, Satan Claus had placed a slimy, rotting hand over each of their mouths. Their chests pulsated violently and their eyelids fluttered furiously, as their souls were sucked out by the creature.

It then lowered them gently to the ground, before carrying them one by one to a bench at the side of the church. The couple were propped up next to each other and looked as though they were asleep, rather than dead. There were no marks on them, no blood and no signs of foul play whatsoever.

Satan Claus, with its red eyes burning brightly, returned to the front door of the church and entered quietly. It had many souls to collect tonight.

* * *

"Come on Jess, wake up!" Davey urged his sister. "Wake up! It's Christmas!"

The first signs of daylight filtered down through the trees, through the window and through the pale curtains in the children's bedroom. They had decided to share a bedroom over Christmas, as their parents knew that Megan would insist on having the third bedroom in the house to herself. There had been a bit more sibling rivalry than normal, but generally the two younger children had been good. The threat from their parents that Father Christmas might not bring any presents if they argued too much had apparently worked.

Jessica opened her eyes and raised her head slowly off the pillow, still in a daze.

"Come ON!" Davey was almost begging now. "We have presents to open."

"Oh, goody," Jessica suddenly became more alert, having realised what day it was. She sprung from her bed and grabbed her brother's hand. They ran out of the bedroom and down the hall to the lounge room.

In their parents' bedroom, Brad and Leonie smiled at each other. It was the same every year. After a few minutes, they got out of bed and made their way to the lounge room as well. "Merry Christmas!" they shouted in unison as they entered the room.

The kids jumped from the floor where they had been taking it in turns guessing what was in the brightly coloured presents, ran to their parents and wrapped their arms around them.

"Let's open the presents. Let's open the presents," Davey and Jessica chanted.

"Oh, coffee first, coffee first" Leonie pleaded, mimicking their chant.

"Pick one present and open that quickly," Brad said. "Then you can play with that while your Mum and I make our coffees and your fruit juice."

Apart from one pile of presents beneath the back of the Christmas tree, it wasn't long before the family had finished opening their presents.

"When are we going to get Megan?" Jessica asked. "I bet she can't wait to open her presents."

"In a couple of hours. In the meantime, you have a lot of new things to play with. How about having a go at this?" Leonie unpacked the Junior Monopoly that Davey and Jessica had wanted for months and they all sat down together to play it.

* * *

A few streets away, another family was enjoying Christmas, sitting under their pergola and eating a breakfast of barbequed eggs, bacon, sausages, tomatoes and mushrooms. This was becoming a tradition for some families in the neighbourhood. The summer days were often too hot in the afternoon to have a roast cooking in the oven. They heard a gate swing open and what they thought was a man in a dirty Father Christmas suit entered their backyard.

"Hey look," a small boy yelled and pointed. "It's Santa!"

"I didn't think your ex was coming around until after lunch." The man looked at his wife accusingly.

"Nor did I," she responded. "Hey, John, aren't you a bit early?"

There was no reply as the gate clanged shut.

"Mummy," the small boy's voice quivered. "I don't think that's the real Santa."

Satan Claus approached them and the rest of the family soon found out what the small boy meant. This

Santa had horrible grey skin, fiery-red eyes and bugs crawling over its dirty suit. Worst of all was its crazy and mostly toothless grin.

"What do you want? If you're here to cause trouble, I'll give you some." The man stood up and approached Satan Claus. Satan Claus raised one arm to head height as the two got closer and tried to place its hand over the man's mouth. The man blocked it and threw a punch at Satan Claus, hitting the creature on the bridge of its nose. It didn't flinch at all.

Satan Claus grabbed the man by the arm, swung him high over its head and sent him flying through the air, before he crashed into one of the poles holding up the pergola. The man's arm was still in the grip of Satan Claus. The man's wife began screaming in terror. Blood spurted from the hole in his shoulder onto the pavers, the garden and the food on the outdoor table. Blood spattered his wife's face and her screaming intensified.

She was stuck to her chair, but the kids jumped up and ran inside the house. Satan Claus walked up to her and placed its hand over her wide-open mouth. The screaming ceased almost immediately and her chest convulsed as her soul was sucked out and into the possession of the demonic beast. As it withdrew its hand, the dead woman slumped back in her chair.

"You bastard," the man croaked with his final breath. Satan Claus rushed across to him to collect his soul, but was too late. The man died too soon. A strange sensation ran through the creature. It was not human, or even alive, but it was scared. It had failed to collect a soul and its Master, the Devil himself, was sure to be unhappy about that.

Satan Claus entered the house, found the kids and gathered their souls, before continuing its journey through the town, searching for as many souls as possible before Christmas ended.

* * *

Megan sat on a bench with her head in her hands at Melbourne's Southern Cross bus station, waiting for the driver to let them all on board. She had a splitting headache from the previous night's shenanigans and wasn't looking forward to the trip back home. She just wanted to return to the boarding school and to her bed.

When they were finally allowed on the bus, Megan walked all the way up the aisle to a seat at the back and spread herself out. She lay impatiently, waiting for the rest of the passengers to take their seats, and felt the bus lurch forward once everyone was ready. A few turns later, the bus left the station and it hadn't even left the CBD before Megan fell asleep.

* * *

After opening their presents and having breakfast, Davey and Jessica played with their new toys for a while, before the family travelled to the bus station to pick up Megan.

"Can you believe how quiet it is?" Brad asked Leonie. "Where are the kids on their new bikes or playing cricket in their new kit? No one seems to be going anywhere for lunch either."

"Weird."

They turned another corner and approached the church where the midnight mass had started about twelve hours earlier. "Look at all the cars parked at the church. I didn't know that a midday mass was happening."

"I'm pretty sure there isn't. Hey, that young couple that opened the new arts and crafts store just down from the supermarket are sitting on the bench. They look like they are asleep."

The family continued on to the bus station and still didn't see anyone along the way. They arrived a few minutes before the bus from Melbourne and while they knew that two other people were arriving at the same time as Megan, there was nobody else waiting at the bus station.

When the bus pulled up, three girls got off, the last one was Megan. The first two were talking and turned to wave to Megan. She ignored them completely and mumbled to her parents, "Hi Mum. Hi Dad."

"Hello darling," Leonie wrapped her arms around her daughter.

The embrace wasn't returned. "Do you have to embarrass me?"

"You are my daughter. Why wouldn't I want to hug you? And you could have said goodbye to your old mates."

"They are idiots and I want nothing to do with them. I'm only here because it's stupid Christmas."

"Don't let your younger brother and sister hear you say that," Brad scolded. "You should know how much they have looked forward to seeing you and sharing Christmas with you. Don't bring them down with you."

Megan scowled. "Yeah, it's great to see you too." She bumped her Dad on the way to the car before turning around. Her parents were looking at her unfavourably. Megan's scowl intensified into a glare. "Can we just go?"

They all got into the car and Megan gathered up as friendly a greeting as she could manage for Davey and Jessica. Arguments and coldness continued part of the way from the bus station to their house, before Brad and Leonie decided not to talk at all.

Brad turned the final corner into their street and Leonie broke the uncomfortable silence. "Hey, there *is* actually somebody around. Look, there's Mr Sutton dressed as Santa. He looks dirty."

"Where? I can't see him," Megan said sourly.

"You probably weren't even watching, Megan."

"Rubbish, Mum. But did his front door just open on its own?"

"You're not seeing straight. All of the alcohol and drugs you have been taking must have fried your brain," Brad remarked, as he pulled the car into their driveway.

"I hate you. I wish I'd stayed in Melbourne." Megan jumped out of the car almost before it had stopped and stormed to the side gate of the house. She pulled it open and continued to the small rotunda in the backyard. Away from the accusing eyes of her parents and questioning eyes of her siblings, she sat on the floor and burst into tears.

"That wasn't a very smart thing to say," Leonie chided her husband as they walked into the house.

"I didn't hear you saying anything to make the situation better." Brad turned briefly to Davey and Jessica. "Go and play with your toys, kids. Your Mum and I have some sorting out to do."

The two youngest children knew that something wasn't quite right, but didn't ask any questions. They decided to pick one of their Christmas presents each and go outside to show Megan.

Megan heard hurrying footsteps and the high-pitched voices of her younger brother and sister. She quickly dried her eyes and greeted them with the brightest smile that she could muster. "They are great presents," she said, as Davey and Jessica took turns to show Megan what they had brought outside.

"I made something for you, Megan," Davey boasted proudly. He took her hand. "Come inside and I can show you what it is."

"Okay. I am sure I will love it."

Davey beamed at Megan and the three of them walked into to the house and to the living room. Their parents were there as well.

"There!" Davey pointed to the sock that had Megan's name on it.

She also saw the cross that her little brother had made. Megan turned on her parents. "How could you let him make such crap when you know I don't believe in religion anymore?"

"Davey made it at school and he doesn't know about your problems," Brad said. "You should show him more consideration. At least thank him for his efforts."

Megan just wanted to scream at her Dad, but guilt rose from the depths of her stomach. She knew it wasn't her brother's fault and she turned to Davey. But it was too late. It was his turn to burst into tears and go out to the backyard. Jessica followed close behind.

* * *

Satan Claus had left Mr Sutton's house with another three souls collected and had seen a car go by. It had watched the car go up the driveway of a house only a few blocks away and it knew it had time to search the other houses in between for souls before getting to that one.

Jessica and Davey looked up as they heard the side gate squeak open. They watched what they thought was Father Christmas come into their backyard. "It's Santa! It's Santa," Davey shouted excitedly, forgetting the troubles that his cross had contributed to.

Satan Claus walked towards them and its maniacal grin widened. As it got closer to the children, they realised that something wasn't right. This Santa was dirty and had bugs crawling out of its mouth. It also had strange red eyes. It entered the rotunda and reached out for Jessica. Davey jumped up and over the banister as

Satan Claus lifted Jessica up with one hand and placed its other hand over her mouth.

"Mummy! Daddy!" Davey screamed desperately. "Santa's got Jessica!" He looked back and watched his sister go limp in Satan Claus's arms.

The parents ran out of the house. "Hey, what are you doing with our daughter?" Brad yelled.

Satan Claus looked at them and grinned more wildly than before. It lowered Jessica gently to the ground, having collected her soul, and watch the two adults as they approached.

Davey looked on from the corner of the house, near the side gate, as the naughtiest Father Christmas that he had ever seen killed his parents. Megan watched from the kitchen window as her parents appeared to have seizures and then collapse slowly to the floor of the rotunda. She could not see Satan Claus. She heard Davey scream and the side gate slam, before the boy ran off down the street.

Megan ran out of the back door towards the bodies of her sister and parents. Satan Claus watched her approach and knew that there was something different about this person. Her soul couldn't be collected. It looked at her as she checked whether her family members were still alive. Megan cried more and more uncontrollably as she discovered, one by one, that they were dead.

* * *

A few hours later, Megan woke up with her head resting on the silent and stable chest of her Father. After shedding another round of tears, she gathered herself, stood up and went in search of her brother. She called out both Davey's name and a more general call of hello as she walked the streets. There was no one around at all.

Megan walked past the house where she knew one of the town's doctors lived and, needing both help to find her brother and an explanation for the deaths of her other family members, she backtracked a few steps and knocked on the front door. A few moments later, she heard footsteps and the door opened. A tall man, around sixty years old with grey hair and a beard, was standing in front of her.

"Oh! Hello Megan. Merry Christmas. I haven't seen you for ages."

"Hi, Doctor Townsend," she managed to say, before bursting into tears.

Doctor Townsend led Megan inside and listened to her explain in fits and starts what had happened and in particular that her parents and sister were dead and that Davey was missing.

Megan and Doctor Townsend walked the streets for over an hour looking for Davey. During that time, they noticed and commented on how unusually quiet the town was; especially for Christmas. Eventually, the two returned to Megan's home and they walked straight to the rotunda, where the bodies of her parents and sister were still laying.

Doctor Townsend investigated all three bodies and became more and more confused as he checked each one. "I am very sorry Megan. As you know, your family is dead, but I don't know how. There are no signs of anything being wrong, apart from that their hearts have stopped. And they could not possibly have all died from heart attacks at the same time."

Megan was about to respond when the side gate squeaked and Davey came charging into the backyard. "Help me," he called breathlessly.

Davey and Megan ran to each other and embraced. "You're okay now," Megan said.

But then the side gate squeaked again and Satan Claus came through it for the second time. "There it is! There it is!" yelled Davey, pointing. He pulled away from Megan and ran to the rotunda.

"What's there? I can't see what you're talking about."

"What?" the doctor asked. "Have you gone blind? There is a devil in a Father Christmas suit."

"Oh, not you too!"

Satan Claus strode straight past a disbelieving Megan and rapidly approached the man, with its hands outstretched. Doctor Townsend tried to retreat, but stumbled and fell to the ground. Satan Claus was on him in a flash and covered his mouth with its hand. Davey screamed as Megan watched the doctor writhe around on the ground for no apparent reason. But she did know that he was in trouble. It was like what happened to Jessica and her parents. She also knew that there was very little she could do.

Doctor Townsend's convulsions stopped and Satan Claus rose with an more deranged grin than ever. Another soul collected and another one to collect. Davey's screaming intensified as the beast approached him. He tried to run but couldn't move. He looked at his sister pleadingly as he cowered.

Megan still couldn't see Satan Claus and didn't understand what was going on, but she ran across the backyard and into the rotunda just as Satan Claus put its hand to Davey's mouth. She saw him thrash around uncontrollably for a few moments, before she grabbed her brother and lifted him up.

The connection between Satan Claus and Davey's soul was broken as Megan pulled him away, just in time. Davey's soul remained with him and he quickly regained consciousness. Realising that his sister was holding him, he clung on as tight as he could.

He heard a loud hissing noise, like gas being released from a valve. Out of the corner of one eye, Davey watched dozens of small lights emerge from Satan Claus's mouth and shoot away in all directions. Four of the lights travelled only a small distance. Two lights went to his Mum and Dad. Another light went to his sister, Jessica. The last of the lights went to Doctor Townsend. These lights entered the four dead people through their noses. Then, moments later, all four coughed a few times, before they sat up dazed and confused.

Satan Claus also watched the lights disappear and the resurrection of the four people it had collected souls from. For the first time since emerging from the hole in the ground in the graveyard behind the church, it wasn't grinning. The fiery redness of its eyes faded. It had lost the souls it had collected and with the source of its energy gone, the demonic creature slumped to the ground and crawled slowly away.

Everyone in the small town had their lives restored, apart from the few people who were actually killed by Satan Claus in the process of it taking their souls.

* * *

Later that night, Brad, Leonie, Megan, Davey and Jessica all sat around the dining room table. It was well past the usual bed time for the smaller children, but they were playing a game of Junior Monopoly.

"You've landed on my square again, Megan," Jessica boasted.

"Oh no, I have to hand over more money," Megan said with a broad smile. "That's me out. I have no money left." She waved her arm at the empty piece of dining room table in front of her.

Brad and Leonie looked at each other happily. They didn't know exactly what had gone on earlier in the day. All they could remember is that, one moment, they had been arguing in the kitchen and the next they had woken up in the backyard. But it had been a wonderful evening. There were no arguments with Megan and all of the kids were getting along well.

Davey had his turn, with the same result as Megan. More money was handed to the younger sister.

"I declare Jessica the winner!" Brad announced.

"Yippee!" The small girl clapped her hands.

After tucking Davey and Jessica into bed, their parents and big sister sat in the living room together. "I'll go on the bus company's website tomorrow and get my ticket changed," Megan said. "Going back New Year's Eve is too soon. I would rather spend more of my holiday here with you, where I should be."

* * *

Dong! The final chime rang through the small church and into the town. Christmas was over for another year. A defeated Satan Claus fell into the hole it had emerged from twenty four hours earlier. There was a low rumble, as the hole in the graveyard behind the church closed up…

X-MAS SECRETS

STEVEN GEPP

I don't think anybody understands why I do what I do. For the past four years I have hired a small shack two miles out of Aldinga and spent the Christmas-New Year's break there, shut away from the rest of the world. In fact, I don't think they really know where I go...

They surely would not suspect that it is here.

She's out there somewhere.

No, I suppose I'm selling my friends and family a little short here. They know why I don't like this time of the year any longer, two weeks after my birthday. But I know they simply can't understand. They don't know the truth.

They think Kloe died on Christmas Day 1994.

They think she was killed in a freak accident four years ago today.

They don't understand that I lost her... That she chose a life I could never hope to provide. That she left me when I had failed...

No... how pathetic of me.

I'm sort of blaming her for all of this. But it was not her fault. Not entirely. Yes, it was her idea. But yes, I went along with it...

We made a deal we should not have made...

And then I did a stupid thing. I broke one of the rules... and I lost out altogether.

It was our fifth Christmas together, that year of 1994. I first asked Kloe to be my girlfriend on October seventh 1989, the day our one week study break for the matriculation exams started. She said yes four weeks later, the day after her final exam. Those dates are there, etched forever in my mind. Childhood sweethearts. Almost. I suppose. But I had been infatuated by her since she had dated one of my friends the previous year and so three months after they broke up I finally gathered the courage to make my move. And it paid off.

That year, to the disappointment of our families, we went off to spend Christmas Day alone. I rented a holiday shack just out of Aldinga. That and the present I bought her used nearly all the money I'd saved during the year working at that damned supermarket - and we drove down to spend two days all alone. Two glorious days.

I'll never forget them. We both lost our virginity. And we were so much in love.

It was incredible.

And then came Life.

We both managed to get into university - and both at Adelaide University. I started my Science degree, and Kloe her arts degree which would see her specialise in psychology over the next few years, also indulging her love of Classics. And we stayed together. Now, I'm not saying everything was perfect. I was first to be unfaithful when I got drunk at a party and ended up sleeping with a girl who I knew had eyes for me. It took Kloe a few months to forgive me for that. A year later Kloe and I started to drift apart, and then I discovered that a guy studying with her had been pestering her to go out with him and she decided to try it.

It took me a long time, but I wooed her back. I used all the romanticism and love and tenderness she had accused me of losing while I was becoming a scientist.

And we made up that year - 1993 - just in time for our annual journey to Aldinga where we rented the same shack - this time for a fortnight - and spent almost the entire time in bed together.

And then came 1994 and our fifth anniversary, as we liked to call it.

I like to think I was going to ask her to marry me during that week... but it never quite happened...

We arrived at the shack on the twenty-fourth and everything went wrong from there...

No. No, it didn't.

I would never have asked her to marry me. That was just something I told people to garner more sympathy. The truth was it was the last roll of the dice for both of us.

I'm trying to find some-one to blame again. For the first time, things were not going well when we arrived at Aldinga. There was still that break-up between us over a year earlier, and the fact that things had fallen back into the same pattern once we had returned from our annual holiday, and the fact that she had actually been with some-one else hanging in the air between us. Now, I don't mean that to sound as though she just decided one day to go off with another man. We had changed, and not all of it for the better.

And maybe that break had done us a world of good. Or maybe this reconciliation was just a case of us deluding ourselves after a year of rather uncomfortable tension. On the journey to Aldinga we chatted and joked and talked, and stopped off at the same roadhouse where we always did and had something to eat, and even made out behind the service station before heading off again.

Just like old times. Perfect.

Until we arrived at the shack late that afternoon...

We walked in carrying our luggage and while I stowed it in the bedroom she went out to the kitchen to make us each a cup of tea. As she stood waiting for the water to boil I came up behind her, grabbed her around the waist and kissed her on the neck, pushing my body against hers.

She wormed sideways out of my grasp.

"What's...?" I started to ask, but the look in her eyes warned me against saying anything further.

"Is that all you ever think about?" she asked, not

bothering to conceal the anger in her voice.

"What?" I repeated stupidly.

"What do you think?" she retorted, turning back to the electric jug chugging away merrily to itself on the kitchen bench.

"Fine," I muttered and went out to sit in one of the chairs set up on the front veranda of the three-room shack.

I stared out across the sea. The shack had been all I could afford five years ago, and while I could easily have hired one larger and closer to the city, I sort of liked the seclusion out here. It was set on the top of a two metre cliff with a set of rickety, weather-worn old stairs leading down to a small stretch of sand, and then the cold waters of the Southern Ocean. The nearest shack was a further kilometre south, while north of us, a kilometre and a half away, the first shacks that made up the outskirts of Aldinga started. We were quite literally all alone in the middle of nowhere. And that was something that only changed in the past year, when the owner of this shack sold some of his land for an exorbitant amount of money, so there are now new structures less than fifty metres away. But not back in 1994.

Apparently, earlier in 1994 - April or May - there was an explosion in Aldinga when an entire house just blew up. The people who had been staying here did not even realise anything was wrong until they went into town for supplies two days after.

And that was what I liked...

Now, after our little exchange, it looked like it was

going to be a long two weeks.

In the end, though, our stay did not even last two days.

Kloe emerged a few minutes later and placed my cup of tea beside me before sitting on the other chair set up out there. I looked over and saw that she had the latest copy of some magazine in her hands. "Thanks," I said.

She looked up at me, then shrugged. "Sure," she muttered, dropping her eyes back to the page.

"What's wrong?" I ventured carefully.

She sighed and, without looking up, muttered, "Nothing."

"C'mon, honey, I..."

"Don't push it. Please," she said earnestly. "Let's just see what happens while we're here."

"Why did you come?" I asked suddenly.

"What do you mean?" She finally rested the magazine on her lap and looked at me.

"You don't want to be here. So why did you come?"

She closed her eyes and sighed. "Phil, I'm not sure if I want to be with you or not," she explained slowly. "I *do* want to be here, but I don't know if I want to be here as your partner. Not anymore. I think we should take this time to examine where we are and where we're headed. Next year I finish my Masters at uni. You've still got three years left before you finish your PhD. We're heading down different paths. We're not the same people we were back in high school. Maybe there is a chance for us or maybe there isn't. I don't know. This past year has been... uncomfortable. For both of us. So let's take this time to see where we are."

"How do we find out?" I asked. I thought I sounded hopeful and eager to continue this relationship with her, but I think I probably sounded angry.

She merely stared at me and shrugged. Then she went back inside.

I sank in the chair. I felt like a weight had been dropped on me from a great height. And I focused all my attention on the sea spread out before me, raising my feet to rest them on the railing. I tried so hard to clear my mind and not to think about anything that before I knew it the sun was casting its deep red glow across the clear sky. It looked like a painting, reminding me once again why I still went there, apart from the tradition Kloe and I had built up between us. And I smiled despite myself as I watched the glowing orb sink behind the gently lapping waves until the only light came from the few street lamps, the myriad of stars and a single light inside the house.

I could hear Kloe rattling around in the kitchen, preparing something to eat. I automatically assumed it was for the two of us, but then decided that probably would not be the case. She always made me fend for myself when she was angry with me. Something I had had a lot of experience with in the previous twelve months. And she sure seemed angry. But I decided to sit a while longer and let her finish before I re-entered the shack. I was depressed. I guess that was it. I was not angry, not upset, just depressed. I think I had known this was coming, and the reality of it all had just hit me.

And then she screamed.

A long, shrill sound that I had heard only once before, when she had been attacked by a dog while we were out walking one afternoon years earlier.

The marrow in my spine froze cold and it took all my will to sprint to her side. She was staring out of the window, pointing with a shaking hand. "What is it?" I asked anxiously. "What's wro…"

She spun and collapsed into my arms. Literally collapsed. I hefted her up and carried her as carefully as I could to the double bed where I laid her gently. "Kloe?" I asked softly. "Are you okay?"

She stirred a little and I brushed the hair out of her face. Her eyes flickered and she looked at me and for the briefest instant I thought she was going to explode again. It was there in her face - accusing me, angry. But it faded as soon as her vision cleared and she just looked at me. "Did you see him?" she asked, her voice started as the little girl's voice I remembered from high school before it became more mature and deeper and somehow rougher. I was so in love with the memory, not the reality… That was unfair. I *was* in love with the girl with me. It was just that I sometimes missed the girl she used to be - with the carefully styled shoulder-length hair, the absence of make-up, the little girl mannerisms tempered with maturity beyond her age that had always set her apart from the others. Now she was an adult and at times so dissimilar it might as well have been two different people. "Did you?" Her pleading voice broke into my memories.

"Did I see who?" I asked carefully, sitting a little

away from her, to give her some space. But her hand snaked forward and grasped mine tight, her fingers locking around mine almost painfully.

"That man." Her eyes searched mine but she could see only concern there, and her grip tightened a little more. "He was looking in through the kitchen window at me…"

"What?" I was on my feet in a flash. After everything that had happened so far today, I was not prepared for an intruder to make matters worse than they already were. "I didn't see anyone while I was out the front on the chair. So he must have come from the back." And I started to leave the room.

"Where are you going?" she asked, gripping my hand.

"To see if he's still out there."

"Please, don't leave me," she whimpered, and it was the Kloe I remembered from our first dates together, the girl who loved me and needed me and wanted me. I stared at her and then sat on the bed beside her. She wrapped her arm automatically around my waist and held onto me with her cheek resting on my shoulder. I placed a soft kiss on the top of her head and held her tight, not daring to do anything else, just waiting for her to feel more relaxed… for things to be the way they always should have been…

-[*]-

It was after nine when we sat down to eat. Kloe's pre-prepared food had spoiled a little so we drove into town and picked up a take-away pizza - something we were sure had not been available the last time we had been here. We sat out the front, watching the waves crash against the beach in the moonlight. We ate pizza and drank Pepsi and laughed and talked again, sharing stories of friends we both knew and things we had both seen. Both of us studiously avoided talking about ourselves and our own shared adventures. It's not that the subject did not come up occasionally, it was just that when it did one of us would automatically talk about something or some-one else. It wasn't just Kloe; I was as guilty as she was. At least we were happy again, sitting beside one another, talking, touching…

The appearance of one strange guy and suddenly we were kids again, eating junk food, giggling, carrying on… having sex…

We had had sex because she wanted to be near me after she had seen that face. It was hollow. I guess that was when I accepted, deep down, that this weekend would be a goodbye weekend. I just did not know exactly how final that goodbye would turn out to be. But in the moment, sitting together, everything was returning to normal.

Then the old man made his appearance.

One moment we were staring out across a sky festooned with stars and dominated by the glowing orb of the moon, the next a face was in front of us.

Kloe screamed and grabbed me. I felt my body grow tense, but my mind was sharp and angry. How dare this man intrude on us! "What?" I spat rudely.

"Seen my dog?" he drawled. His face showed he had not shaved for a few days and his clothes were in need of a wash, but the look in his eyes was incredibly sad. "Small and brown. Black collar."

"I haven't seen a dog all night," I said, calming my voice and offering what I hoped was a smile.

"And we're eating out here, so he would've smelt it and come sniffing around, I guess," Kloe added. "Maybe he's down on the beach."

"Maybe he is. Well, thanks," the old man muttered. "Sorry for disturbing you."

"I hope you find your dog," I offered as he walked away.

"So do I," he said as he faded into the blackness.

We watched him go, both feeling a little sad for him. Then: "Was that the man you saw?" I asked.

Kloe smiled, then burst out laughing before controlling herself.

"What's so funny?' I asked.

"No, not him," she said, smiling.

"Well, I didn't see him," I countered. "What did your fella look like, then?"

She paused and thought briefly. "Well, for one thing, he was young. Our age or maybe a little older. He had a beard, but a short and very neat. His face and shoulders were muscular. His eyes…" Her voice started to drift a little. "His eyes were very blue. And he was not wearing a top. His hair was dark, over his shoulders." She stared at me, and her face was curious. "In fact, I'd say he was quite good looking."

I laughed. "So why did you scream?"

"He frightened me," she replied, a little hurt.

"Fair enough," I agreed, trying to smooth the situation. I realised that if I was going to be on tenterhooks for the whole holiday then this was not going to be a fun trip for me. "So you were scared, but he did not look threatening."

"Yeah," she agreed, snuggling back under my arm. "That's right." But there was something to her tone of voice and the way her eyes stared straight ahead that had me concerned but I could not for the life me work out what that was…

-[*]-

The red numbers on the old digital clock beside the bed said that it was now not quite two o'clock in the morning on Christmas Day. Merry Christmas. Ho, ho, ho. Or, as Kloe would have written it - Merry X-mas. One of her little foibles... and since that day I have not been able to bear looking too long at things spelt like that at Christmas time. At the time I thought it was cute, now it is a conduit for bad memories. Just seeing the word X-mas on a sign for a Christmas sale brings back so many emotions that I often flee the store. Again, no one quite understands why...

But there I was. It was two o'clock in the morning of December twenty-fifth, 1994. Beside me, with her back to me, Kloe was sleeping soundly. I still loved to listen to the deep chesty rumble that was her version of snoring. I sat up and stared down at myself, dressed only in my underpants. We had gone to bed before eleven and fallen asleep in each other's arms. No talking, no sex, nothing. Just a hug and then early to sleep. I carefully sat up, rubbed my face and cast one last glance at her before I swung my legs around to the floor.

What had woken me? I wondered absently. I did not remember a dream at all, and I did not need to go to the toilet or get a drink. I sighed and cradled my head in my hands. Maybe it was something as simple as the stress of what was happening between us that had finally got to me, and I had felt her move away, and I had reacted…

But even that wasn't it. Something had physically disturbed my sleep. I stood and walked across to the window. I moved the blinds apart a little and peered out over an expanse of vegetation, with the lights of the next shack barely visible in the distance. The waves crashed at the foot of the cliff and a few crickets chirped into the night. Nothing out of the ordinary. Just the shrubs and bushes and sounds that had been here for as long as I could remember…

I heard it then.

It was the sweetest, softest sound I had ever heard. Its melody floated on the breeze. I had never heard the melody before but it seemed somehow familiar. A voice in the darkness formed words that I could not understand but which made all the sense in the world to me. It was coming from close by, calling me. The only thought that entered my head was that I had to find the source of that music and be with it. I walked out through the front door and down the steps to the beach below.

The wind was surprisingly cold and it bit into me like a thousand tiny fangs, but I did not stop. It was as though my body was not my own. I was under the control of the strange musical voice. It was coming from down by the water's edge. I walked until I was standing knee-deep in the freezing sea.

Then the music stopped.

And so did I.

The full force of the elements hit me and I almost collapsed as the freezing water and chilled air hit my senses. I bolted out of the water and stood on the beach, shivering, rubbing my arms and moving about on the spot, wondering just what in the hell I was doing out there. I thought I heard a shrill scream and I turned to face the cliff and the shack on top of it where I had just come from. Kloe... But the scream stopped as suddenly as it had begun... and I no longer recognised it. But surely it had been...

Been...

And then the soft hand touched my elbow. I jumped and spun quickly, moving back a few steps as fast as I could.

The eyes that greeted me were smiling without any hint of malice. They were large and blue, wide and deep, staring at me from beneath a mane of thick dark hair that reached down to the knees of her naked body, with her alabaster white skin glowing in the pale moonlight. She smiled and her lips parted a little to reveal perfect pearl-white teeth. She reached out a hand and again touched me on the arm with her delicate fingers and she opened her mouth.

The song that came forth was so full of pure emotion - joy, love, sadness, everything all swirling in and out within one another like a maelstrom of such strong feelings that I almost cried…

Her arms were wrapped around me and the song filled my head. The feelings she sang to me were made physical and the sensations were like nothing I had ever felt before…

I was in paradise…

Nothing else mattered...

Nothing...

...and no one...

-[*]-

I crept back into the house and did not even look at Kloe before climbing back into the bed. I was no longer cold, and I could feel the smile etched onto my face. I decided it had to be a dream; things like that just did not happen...

But as I slid beneath the single sheet beside the girl I had brought here with me, not even considering her at all, a wave of guilt washed over me. I could feel a knot in my stomach building up, threatening to come out, choking me with bile and tears...

What had I just done with an unnamed lady on the sands of Aldinga beach?

I finally cast a glance at the lover I had come here with, the woman I had not even thought about before accepting the embrace of the singing vision of loveliness on the shore…

Kloe was on her back. Some time while I was gone, she had discarded her top, revealing her small breasts and the appendix scar I so loved to run my finger down when we had first started dating. Her hair fell in waves across one shoulder, longer now than I could ever remember seeing her wear it, looking like something out of a photo shoot. And, on top of all that, there was a slight smile on her lips. She was the vision of a sleeping princess, lovely and young, as though the past five years had never happened.

There was no hint of anything that would have made her scream... Had I imagined that? Had I imagined everything? Was this really just a dream? No, the feelings still in my body told me just how real it had all been...

And I felt guiltier than ever as I rolled over away from her, sure that the smell of the sea was coming from myself and not the open window beside our bed…

-[*]-

I was awake first and set about making breakfast after preparing the room as we always did on Christmas Day. A Christmas/X-mas Day together. *Another* X-mas Day together.

And I was starting it feeling full of remorse.

I had to make up for it...

Granted, when I had first awoken and climbed into the shower I had thought the previous night had just been some strange male sex fantasy - the sea nymph come forth from the waves to seduce and take the young man. But the strong odour of the ocean that still hung in the air was something that I could not deny. I tried to wash it off, but it stayed there like a curtain that had fallen over me and everything I had wanted this time away to be.

I really had to make up for it.

I heard the shower start in the back of the shack, accompanied by the vibrating of the pipes in the walls where the hot water system had never quite been fixed properly and smiled a little. Kloe was awake and moving. I hoped she put that smell down to a strong wind or something else and did not ask too many questions. I do not know how I would have answered them with the way I was feeling that morning... but why should she ask any questions at all? Why should she even suspect anything? She had even been smiling when I had returned to bed, and if she asked where I had been I would simply say I went for a walk along the beach because I had to clear my head.

That would work. Satisfied with myself and my planned lies, I returned to my culinary work.

"Smells good." I jumped a little. I had not even heard the shower stop running, let alone Kloe's entry.

"Thanks," I replied as she came up behind me and hugged me around the stomach. She placed a kiss on my neck and then peered over my shoulder - just what she had objected to me doing the previous day. Maybe a good night's sleep was all we needed. Or...

"And thank-you for the Christmas present," she whispered before walking off to get plates and cutlery ready.

"You deserve it," I responded, unable to hide my joy. She had found the small parcel wrapped in plain paper I had placed upon the pillow beside her head. The necklace within had cost me a lot but I felt that that was my last attempt at rescuing this relationship, and whatever I spent it was worth it.

That's all I have now...

I eventually carried the breakfast to the table and

served it up. She had placed a card in front of my place. Written in her neat handwriting, as always, was: *Our X-mas*. And the card contained the same lines she always wrote. "Another X-mas, another year." I read it and smiled.

"Thanks," I whispered.

She smiled briefly at me but said nothing. We ate in silence, and a slightly uncomfortable silence at that. I avoided her gaze, but it seemed to me she avoided looking me in the eyes as well. I put it down to the fact that she had apparently not gotten me a Christmas present, but I ignored it. Gifts and cards were not what this time together was about - salvaging our lives was far more important. And so I made nothing of it. After we finished, she cleaned up the dishes while I cleaned the kitchen itself and then I suggested we go for a morning walk along the beach, as we had that very first Christmas Day together.

She paused only briefly before agreeing, and so we headed down the stairs at the side of the cliff to the wet sand.

We talked and we chatted and it was just like the previous night, where we talked about everything except that which we really should have talked about - us. Oh sure, we talked about the past, reminiscing about Christmases past, parties, high school, mainly our first few years together, but not anything we should have been discussing. Not where we were at that time, not where we were heading... not what had happened in the past year, not the other people who had entered our lives, not where we saw ourselves now and into the future. We were chatting; we were not talking. But, at the time, it was exactly what we had to do.

It is just a shame we never got a chance to take that next step.

Because what happened next changed our lives forever.

For then we saw them.

They came walking out of the sea, both naked, the water dripping off them in a slight mist, giving them a surreal halo. He was a muscular man with a short beard and long dark hair, looking more like some sort of Renaissance depiction of a god than any man I could have imagined.

And she...

She was the one I had seen on the beach the previous night, looking even more gorgeous than my memory had allowed me to think.

And they were coming directly towards us, their arms around one another's waist, their grins as wide as the ocean stretched out before us, their blue eyes fixed upon us.

I turned and looked at Kloe. Her face registered the same shock I was feeling, and I turned back to the two smiling people still steadily coming towards us. We could not move a muscle.

"Ah, greetings, my two young lovers," the man said, and I noticed the hint of a Mediterranean accent in his deep voice.

"Do we know you?" I asked as emotionlessly as I could manage.

He laughed and shook his head. "Ahh, the secrets of

the young," he mused. "No, *you* do not know me, but your lovely partner here does." He paused and his piercing blue eyes bore right into my own, making me feel uncomfortably like a small child, but I was unable to draw my gaze away from his. "She knows me just as you know my own companion," he added coldly, the smile not faltering once.

Kloe jerked away from me and stared at me and I at her. "You..." she started, but stopped herself. Because I could see it there as well - that scream last night had been hers, but then it had stopped. This was the man she had seen at the window. And he had come again. And while I had been on the beach, he had been in the house...

"Secrets," the man went on. "So many of them. And the two of you are quite clearly very good at keeping yours." He threw his head back and laughed. "Until this very moment, you had no idea of what the other did last night. I am indeed impressed. Such secrecy. So strange for ones so young and so devoted."

He paused and stepped closer, staring at our faces intently. "Or is devoted too strong a word?"

Neither of us could say a thing as he folded his arms across that impossibly muscular chest and stared at us, his eyes laughing.

She just stared at us as though we were mildly amusing exhibits in a zoo. Then she faced him and started to sing. Her voice was a musical instrument but the words were completely unintelligible.

He nodded sagely as he listened. Then his smile returned and he opened his arms. "Ahh, my two young lovers. As you are so good at keeping secrets, maybe you would like to share our secret?" he asked, in his booming voice. "And maybe you would like to hear what we have to offer?"

I faced Kloe.

Her face became etched in stone. She gazed at me as though I was a total stranger. She faced him. "Just what is it you have to offer?" she asked him quietly.

I swallowed and shook my head. This was not the way things were supposed to be. We were supposed to be getting our lives back on track, not drifting further apart. "Kloe..." I croaked, but she did not even acknowledge me.

The man's smile managed to get even wider. "After last night's... escapades, yes, I think we have chosen a good couple."

"I don't understand..." I started.

"Shut up, Phil," Kloe said blandly, her eyes not leaving the two before us.

"Here is my offer," he said boldly, hands on his hips, his body looking even more like something dreamed up by an artist, not anything that could possibly be of this world. The woman stood by his side, her body partially hidden by her extraordinarily long hair, her eyes never leaving mine, smiling demurely. "I will take you, Kloe, and my companion will take you, Phil. You are not to ask any questions. You are to do as you are told. You do that until the setting of the sun and you shall have your heart's desire. Break the rules... and you lose all you want most."

I folded my arms across my chest and shook my

head emphatically. “Look, I don’t know who you are or what you want from us, and I don’t think...”

“I agree.” We all fell silent and stared at Kloe. Her face turned to face mine. “We’ve already gone too far. We both know what happened last night...”

I grabbed her hand and led her out of earshot from the two naked people who were staring calmly at us. “What in the hell are you doing?” I hissed.

Her eyes were cold. “We both had an opportunity last night to sleep with some-one else and we both took it,” she growled in return. “You and me. Both of us. This relationship is not what we really want, isn’t that obvious? We’re going through the motions. I feel it, and you surely can’t be dumb enough not to feel it as well. But this man is offering...”

“What he’s offering is impossible,” I countered.

“And what happened last night wasn’t?”

“What do you think this is?” I almost yelled. “Some naked guy comes, says he wants to have sex, and then we get everything we want? Does that sound real? This guy’s a crackpot...”

“Why did you sleep with that woman last night?” she asked suddenly.

I paused, then sighed. “I heard music, and was drawn to her voice...”

“Like you had no control,” she finished for me. “And I heard the sound of the sea, washing over me, lulling me to sleep, but I was awake.” She grabbed my hands and looked into my eyes. “These people are not people. They might be able to give us back what we've lost… what we want."

"I don't know what you're talking about. Who *are* these people?" I blustered.

"I know who they are. And I believe them," she replied, unable to hide her smile.

"Then what...?" I started, but she was already headed back. In the days that followed I thought that her greed had overtaken her... and probably something else. Maybe the memory of what had happened the night before. But as I look back on it now, I really don't know her motivation. Unless she already knew what her heart's desire would be, and had already sown the seeds for our parting.

By the time I had rejoined them the deal was done.

The woman took me by the hand and led me towards the shack while Kloe and the man went off towards a distant place further down the beach. I cast one last glance over my shoulder; Kloe did not even appear to be concerned... and she certainly did not look back in my direction...

And the last image I have of my lover was her of her back, walking along the beach hand in hand with a man who could have been a Greek god.

-[*]-

The girl took me back into the shack, walking up the cliff-side stairs with the grace and ease of a ballet dancer. She paused at the front door and looked all around at the structure. She reached out and touched the railing at the front nervously, then looked back at me. I smiled and waved my hand towards the front door. She touched the entranceway tentatively and it swung open. She paused a little, then took her first steps forwards...

We went inside and she sat at the kitchen table, testing the chair with her feet first. And then she began to look around at her surroundings with a mixture of fear and curiosity. Her eyes took in every detail of the house, poring over the fixtures, the furniture, everything. It was almost as though it was all completely new to her. But I remembered what the man had said and I did not ask her any questions. I just waited, looking at the naked woman in the shack with me, unable to take my eyes from the perfection of her form. Then: "Water, please?"

Her voice was a little croaky, and she clearly struggled with the two simple words she had just spoken, but I got her a glass of water immediately. She swallowed it in one gulp and held out the empty glass. I filled it again and once more she took it all. And now, finally, she smiled and took my hand in hers.

This time she knew exactly where to take me.

-[*]-

We spent the day together. No words were spoken except for her to ask for a drink every so often. And to go to the shower. And it happened regularly. We had been together for only an hour or so when she first asked in her halting, unsure voice, "Where shower please?"

"Right this way," I smiled and led her into the cramped bathroom. Once inside I started to run the shower, thinking about what we could do together beneath the running water, but she stood back against the far wall. "What's wrong?" I asked carefully, walking towards her.

She shied away from my wet hands, her face screwing up into a mask of terror. “No,” she whispered. I stopped immediately. That expression was so fearful that I could not continue. “Me alone,” she murmured. “Please.”

“But I don’t...” I started, then stopped myself. I had to remember not to push my luck here. No matter my doubts about what all of this was, Kloe seemed to have known. She thought she understood... and I was not going to rock the boat. All my desires would be mine if I could survive this most bizarre Christmas Day ever. “Okay,” I muttered and backed out of the room. Almost immediately, the door was shut in my face and locked. I heard the water start up, but the pipes were not vibrating in the walls, so she was not using the hot water. I went back to the kitchen where I poured myself a drink and waited.

It was more than an hour later before she re-emerged, dried and looking as radiant as ever. She smiled at me and took me by the hand. Once more I was led into the bedroom and onto the bed...

Four times it happened. Four times she disappeared to have an hour-long cold shower, and each time I was ushered out of the room, and I waited, biding my time, for her to reappear. The sun moved slowly across the sky, from morning, past noon and into late afternoon. The day could have lasted forever for all I cared.

And we were still together, entwined with one another. She went to the shower and came out and we started anew each time. Even if I could not perform the way I would have liked, that did not stop her nor did she allow it to stop me. She was the most amazing lover I had ever encountered; as responsive and knowledgeable as anybody I have encountered before or since. When she emerged from the shower that fourth time I was waiting for her eagerly.

She came to me, moving with the grace of a snake sliding through long grass. As I laid down she maneuvered herself over the top of me on her hands and knees... then stopped.

She coughed a little, then turned her head and her whole body convulsed as a thin thread of green saliva trickled out of her mouth and onto the floor. I reached up to touch her cheek and literally felt the skin change, growing rougher beneath my touch. It was tough and rubbery, like wet leather. She stared at me in horror and I could actually see the texture of her skin change ever so slightly. "No..." she whispered and once more barricaded herself inside the bathroom and ran the water.

I tried knocking on the door. "Are you okay?" I called urgently. But the only reply was a gurgling sound, a sound of pain and so pathetic that I started to lose control. "Are you all right?" I called, louder and more urgently, and this time I heard the sound of something wet hitting the floor. Something wet and heavy and solid.

That was all I had to hear..

It took me two heavy shoulder hits to crack the door open, sending the chain lock flying across the room.

I knew then that it was all over...

All over for me at least...

For she was laying on the floor underneath the running water of the shower.

But I only recognised her because her face was still the same. The round eyes, full lips, button nose, white skin. But her head... It was covered in orange and brown scales. Her hair had been replaced by seaweed, strands of green string coming from the top of her head. Her arms were shorter and thicker, corded with muscle, her hands webbed and clawed and bigger, her legs gone, replaced by the long, thick tail of some sort of brown-green fish.

She stared up at me then closed her eyes and started to weep. The tears green, the sound a song of depression. I watched the water from the shower cascading over her scaled skin and slowly, surely, her form changed, to take on once again vestiges of the image I had been loving all day long...

But I could bear no more.

I fled into the shadows of dusk...

"I pity you."

I looked around but could see no source for the deep voice that filled my ears. I was sitting at the base of a tree, hugging my knees to my chest, rocking back and forth. Everything was gone... but I did not know how complete that statement would turn out to be. All I could think about was that thing in the bathroom...

"You have broken the rules of our agreement."

"Kloe..." I started, looking all about as the wind rose a little and the deep voice once more echoed through my head.

"Ah, yes. She has succeeded. She has chosen her heart's desire." A laugh faded as the wind died down a little before once again picking up with the voice that spoke on it. “She wants her freedom, and what better freedom than that which I can give her?”

And I was alone...

-[*]-

Her clothes were found on the beach. The necklace I had given her had been placed carefully on top of the pile. The police were especially kind to me.

I found myself reading her card and its X-mas greeting over and over. Our last communication. I held the necklace in my hands...

Then, one day, I went back to Adelaide.

And a year later I came back here.

That’s that.

Because one day I will see her again, out there, living to her heart’s content with the freedom that she was obviously so keen to have... and so keen to have away from me.

She could keep her secret and follow the rules much better than me, but I shall never give up hope of seeing her again.

One day.

One Christmas Day.

One last X-mas Day...

Maybe...

RAINMAKER

KATHRYN HORE

The heat lay across every surface. The lacquered wood of her desk. The sticky leather of her chair. The leather clung to her thighs and hurt as she shifted and pulled skin. Sweat lay against her back, under her blouse, under her breasts, soaking her bra until it was damp against her skin. A simmering heat that open windows and failing air conditioning could not help. There was a small desk fan but it only moved about hot air. A small desk-top plastic Christmas tree, which was meant to look jolly and festive but only seemed as wilted as everything else, failed to sway in the artificial breeze.

The boy didn't seem to notice. Or if he did, he wasn't showing it. He wasn't showing anything.

Dressed in black, heavy boots, dyed hair falling across downturned eyes, scowl. The uniform of a thousand rebellious teenagers. She'd seen it before, in all its variations. It was nothing to be afraid of. He presented different to the photo in the thin slip of a file put together by the court-appointed social worker. It had been a school photograph, maybe a year and a half old, from whatever hick country town school he'd been in at the time. Then he'd been short haired, clean dressed, smiling. Crooked-toothed, but happy. What a difference a year could make at that age.

She looked down at her notes so far. A few scrawls. Useless things made to look like she was paying attention. Words with no purpose. He had said little, only the most perfunctory. It wasn't surprising. Often even the kids who were only there because their parents were over-anxious and not because there was anything actually wrong with them, said nothing in the first session. Or the third. Or the sixth. Sometimes it seemed they all knew the code. Sit sullen and silent until the hour was up.

Sometimes she managed to make a connection.

Sometimes she didn't.

This kid needed her to. He was down to his last chance. She decided to try again.

'So. Jeremy. Do you want to talk about your father?'

Dark eyes flashing. A nerve hit. 'Tell me about your mother,' he mimicked in falsetto, squeaky and mocking. 'Tell me about your childhood.' He lifted his chin, dropped the squeaking. 'Whatever, Sigmund-fucking-Freud. You're the expert. You've got the file. You tell me.'

Obvious aggression; easily ignored. Defensive. Hurting. At least he was saying something. She kept his gaze, not about to let her eyes drop first when he hadn't even looked at her for the first ten minutes he had sat there. She tried to ignore the bead of sweat she could feel trickling down the center of her back and focus instead on him, but the heat was suffocating.

'I'm not an expert. I'm just the one the magistrate appointed to try and keep you out of prison.'

'Juvenile detention,' he corrected, making it clear he knew she used the word for effect.

'It's the same thing, Jeremy.'

He smirked. 'You think?'

She glanced down at her non-existent notes, made a pretense of flicking through the file under them, inspected the first bit of paper to hand. 'It says here you were a straight A student back in Hallsworth –'

'Hallysworth. Get it right.'

'Hallysworth. Excellent school results. Liked by teachers. Worked hard.' She looked up again, tried to meet his eyes, but he was looking away, out the window to the heat-suffocated city beyond. 'So what happened this year?'

'Oh, I don't know. My father died. You reckon that might be it?'

Three days before Christmas last year, stripped off, took a cold shower, then hanged himself in the hayshed while still dripping wet. Found by his only son, fifteen years old at the time, eldest child, two younger sisters, ten and six respectively. A mother who couldn't cope, knocked out on pills or booze, from well before her husband's death. A farm with starving cattle Jeremy had taken his turn at destroying, the last thing he and his father had done together, shotgun to large bovine temples, the cattle too weak to shy away. Land sold for almost nothing, after his father was found wet and swinging. His mother couldn't get it together, State threatening to take the kids. Instead they were dragged here to live in his grandmother's tight, three-bedroom brick-veneer in outer suburban Melbourne, all within a couple of months of his father's funeral.

The file said it all. She'd read it more than once in preparation, looking for clues, looking for a way in. It was certainly enough to screw up a teenage kid. It was enough to screw up anyone.

'You like Southtern East High?' she asked. He only shrugged, a languid, uncaring movement.

'It's alright. Same as anywhere.'

'Same as your school back in Hallysworth?'

A flash of animation in his eyes. If she didn't know better, she would have read it as amusement. 'Nah. That was a shithole. The computers are better here. There are science labs and stuff. They didn't have that back at the old place.'

'So you like this school better?'

'I didn't say that. Only that the resources are better.'

The file didn't actually say it all, of course, despite its extensive, clinical detail of dysfunction and tragedy written stark on the page. Something was missing from the official record of this damaged boy who'd apparently stood and watched as three of his classmates had drowned. Such as how they had managed to drown in a suburban high school toilet block. She'd heard of heads flushed down toilets in high school bullying. She'd never heard of anyone dying from it before.

Someone had appended a copy of the inquest report before sending the file over. It arrived complete with lurid images of the three dead boys. Coroner's findings, water in the lungs, drowning. Which in no way explained photographs of husk like bodies so dried-out they looked half-way to mummification.

Three dead teenagers sucked dry. One dead father, dripping wet in a drought.

'You've been accused of vandalism at the school,' she said, eyes scanning the pages before her. 'Of destroying one of the Food Tech kitchens by deliberately flooding it. A science lab, the same thing.'

'It wasn't me.'

She looked up. 'You've been accused of vandalising bathrooms. Of blocking the plumbing. On one occasion, getting into the mains and turning the water off to the school completely.'

He didn't drop his stare. 'It wasn't me.'

'Before leaving Hallysworth, you hadn't been in trouble with police even once.'

Silence. If anything, he looked bored. She supposed he had heard this before, the litany of his supposed crimes.

'You seem to attract trouble, Jeremy.'

'Did you know the fully grown human body contains on average 40 litres of water?' he said, and the sudden announcement made her shoulders straighten. 'Adult bodies are around sixty to seventy per cent water. Children even more.'

He was changing the subject. But at least he was talking. She could go along with that.

'No, I did not know that.'

'I learnt it in school. In those science labs I'm meant to have destroyed just for the fun of it.' He half smirked, a point scored. 'Actually, I knew it before. Southtern East might have good resources, but the Hallysworth curriculum was way more advanced.'

He leant forward and shifted the desk fan an inch to the right. Immediately, the plastic desk Christmas tree across from it, with its little bits of painted cardboard as ornaments and tiny coloured string for tinsel, began to flutter with the fan's slow turn. Fake presents were propped up underneath, matchboxes painted gold, silver, red, green. Only a week until Christmas. She still had shopping to do, presents, food to buy for the extended family onslaught. They came to her place because she had a pool. Aunts, uncles, cousins, nephews.

Jeremy leant back in his seat again. Black hair falling across his face, all snarls and attitude. Still a sixteen year old boy who this time last year had found his Dad's hanged body. The anniversary of it was only a couple of days away. What sort of Christmas must he be expecting?

'How's your Mum?' she asked on impulse. Would his mother even be able to think of Christmas for the kids? Was Christmas even possible for his family?

'Drunk probably. Why? You stuck on that Freudian-childhood thing again?' he said, cocking his head. 'Why don't you ask what you really want to know?'

'And what would that be, Jeremy?'

'About Davy and his mates. The dead ones. The ones dried out and drowned.'

'Why do you think I want to know about them? I'm here to talk about you.'

'Because that's all anybody wants to know. Either about them or Dad. The dead speak loud.' He was looking away again, out the window to the oppressive blue sky beyond. 'I know because I hear them.'

It took deliberate effort to keep her expression neutral and her hand steady as she wrote a careful note on her pad. This was a kid who had gotten straight As at Hallysworth and straight Cs at Southtern East. Literally straight Cs, his last report card sporting a suspicious uniformity. He was not stupid. If he could engineer exactly the same C-grade in every single class he took, then he could figure out which buttons to press to get a reaction from the authority figures around him. His teachers. The Principal. The police. Her.

Knowing that didn't stop the wash of professional skepticism cross her face.

He turned to roll his eyes at her. 'Don't worry, lady. I'm not about to go all *I see dead people* on you.'

No, but when telling her he heard them, it was the first time he had actually sounded genuine since he had walked in. So was he trying to get a reaction out of her?

Or was the trauma of the past twelve months evolving into something else again?

'Do you mean their stories have become more important than your own?' she suggested, all so gently.

'Jesus, you like your psychobabble, don't you? I said I hear them. I *meant* I hear them. Talking. Whispering. Words.'

'Okay. Well, what words do you hear?'

'Can I have a glass of water?'

It took her a moment to realise he was asking for himself, not telling her what he heard the dead supposedly say. She nodded a perfunctory agreement and had to slip sweating feet back into shoes beneath the desk before she got up. Her toes felt squishy in the low, enclosed heels and her blouse was damp against her back as she moved. She couldn't help but think of the swimming pool at home with some longing. Couldn't help but wonder how much longer she could sit and banter with the boy without getting anywhere.

She asked Sally on reception to fetch the water. Returned to her desk to find Jeremy staring again out of the window. Sally entered behind her, all middle-aged bustle and greying hair, handed the glass to the boy. He murmured a thanks, but just sat there unmoving until Sally was forced to leave again, quizzical glances unanswered.

When the door clicked shut behind the receptionist, Jeremy lifted the glass. But half way to his lips he paused. She watched as he glanced down and stared inside the glass. Hesitated with caught breath. There was a flash of something across his face. Was it guilt? Or despair? Some unbidden memory catching him without warning?

She couldn't shake the thought that it looked more like fear.

It was stupid to read too much into body language. One of the earliest lessons of her career. Sometimes someone crossing their arms wasn't being defensive, they just found it a comfortable way to sit. And sometimes someone who winced and hesitated before drinking a glass of water wasn't afraid, they just had indigestion.

He brought the glass to his lips. Took the slightest of sips. Seemed to breathe deeply a moment, pausing, considering, and only then did he drink more, a real gulp. Taking the plunge and drinking it all, finishing the glass in several long swallows. The kid must have been desperately thirsty. By the time he brought it down again, there wasn't a drop left in the glass.

She waited until he had put the empty glass back on the desk, pushing it well into the middle as if afraid it might fall from the edge, before beginning again.

'Better?' she asked, vaguely wishing she'd asked Sally to bring her a glass as well. Her throat was suddenly parched after watching him drink like that.

Typically, he only shrugged. She let the silence sit there a moment before pushing for more.

'You were saying you hear your father. That he speaks to you.'

'I said I hear the whispers of the dead. I didn't say they were Dad.'

'Who are they then?'

'I don't know. But they're thirsty. Always so fucking thirsty,' he said, his voice dull, as if he knew how it would sound, but found himself saying it anyway. 'It began when the water started running out on the farm. It got worse after we shot the cattle. Whispering about thirst, about other stuff.'

'What other stuff?'

He was unconsciously chewing at his lip. She could all but see the battle of trust, common to every damaged kid who walked into her office, going on behind his eyes. To take the leap, or not. To open up, or not. To trust.

Or not.

'Bringing the rain.'

She took that in, nodding slowly. Made some scratching marks in her notebook for the sake of it. Said, 'I see,' in her most clinical tone. Looked up again to realise he was scowling at her and had the sudden sense of being see-through.

She pushed on quickly.

'Do you believe the voices you hear, Jeremy?'

'I know how it sounds, Doc,' he said. 'I know what you're thinking. Troubled kid hears the dead. I know what it means to you.'

He did not say the word. *Psychosis*. But she wrote it down anyway.

'The thing is,' he said, after enough pause for her to note it all on her pad, 'you're wrong. They wanted the rain. Well, we all wanted the rain. The farm was going to shit and Dad was freaking out. It seemed to make sense. So I did it. I thought, what the fuck, why not try? Only then...'

He trailed off. She tried to swallow but found her throat too dry.

'Only then what, Jeremy?'

'Only then it went wrong. And I knew it was wrong, but I only wanted to bring the rain. I didn't realise what would happen.'

'What did happen?'

'Dad walked in. It wasn't my fault. He didn't understand. I tried to stop it. I really tried –'

He stopped. He shook his head; a slight, tense movement. No more. She tried not to say anything, she wanted him to fill the silence, but for a long moment he seemed to let it stand, as if he was happy to have them sit without sound as the minutes ticked by. A battle of wills, one she almost thought he would win, for she was about to say something when he finally burst out with more.

'It's coming,' he said quickly.

'What's coming?' She spoke just as quick.

'The rain. It's coming. It'll be here in time for Christmas. Any day now. Any minute, maybe.'

His urgency was almost infectious. She made herself sit back and take a long breath through dry lips, deliberately letting his words wash over her to minimise their impact. It was too easy to get caught in the paranoia of another's delusions. She had to keep an emotional distance, a professional distance. So she took pause and looked down at her notes, trying to wet her lips with her tongue, though it was near as dry as they were. She wondered if she still had any lip-balm in the bottom of her handbag.

On her notepad, she scribbled *rain making*, circled it, drew a line from that circle back to an earlier note, *hears dead father*, and circled that too. Jotted at the side, *anniversary of father's suicide*. Paused for a moment, then added *Christmas* next to it.

Considered her notes for a moment and knew she wasn't getting anywhere.

'You know, many would hope you are right,' she said. 'Everyone would love to see the rain come.'

'Not this rain. They won't want this rain.'

'Why not?'

'This is rain without clouds. And rain without clouds has got to come from somewhere else.'

He wanted her to ask where. She resisted, despite the urge to do just that. It was at the center of his delusion, which meant he needed her to buy into it and make it real. She had to admit, he was more coherent than she was used to. They usually rambled more, had less point to their vague assertions of threat. By contrast, Jeremy seemed almost too consistent. Yet the signs were clear. Paranoia, delusions, hearing voices. Traumatic instigation for it all. Classic psychosis. Practically textbook.

He was sitting forward again, with his elbows on his knees, staring at the little Christmas tree. It struck her that she should have thought to move it before his session. The season was not one of joy for Jeremy. Disintegrating families, destroyed farms. Christmas for him would forever be the season of death and loss. Next to that, the tacky cheer of her little plastic tree seemed somehow inappropriate.

'Tell me about the voices, Jeremy. Where do they come from?'

'The drought brought them, I think. They're all the ones who died thirsty and now they're trapped.'

'Why are you the only one who hears them?'

'I'm not. I'm just the only one who listens.' He sounded very matter-of-fact, glancing up momentarily, looking back to the tree. 'Do you know what Davy and his mates were doing in the toilets at school, Doc?'

Changing the subject again. She decided to let him, shaking her head with a, 'no, what?', then trying yet again to swallow. Her throat felt like sandpaper. Maybe she was coming down with something, a summer cold. She hoped not. It was rotten timing, just before Christmas. She made a mental note to go by the chemist on her way home, get some throat lozenges. The last thing she needed right now was to get sick over Christmas.

'They were shitheads,' he told her, as she thought of pharmaceuticals. 'But as far as bullies go, least they were modern. No flushing heads in toilets. That's old-school.' He even uttered a bleak kind of laugh. 'They got their ideas from politics class. Waterboarding, they reckoned. Only way to go in this day and age.'

She felt her face fall. Calculations of which chemist was closest on her route home were banished from her thoughts. It wasn't that she was unfamiliar with the extremities of modern schoolyard bullying; a lot of the kids she saw were either victims or perpetrators, each troubled in their own right. The imagination of childhood, always so potent. But that was a new one. And it took her by surprise.

She tried not to seem too shocked. She was a professional. She tried to take it all in calmly, clinically.

'Did they try it on you, Jeremy? The waterboarding?'

'They were going to. They started to.'

She chose her next words with carefully.

'There were three of them. Two were footy players, athletes,' she said, gently. 'It's okay if you were unable to stop them, Jeremy. You know that, don't you?'

'I did stop them.'

So certain. Her lips felt cracked as she tried to lick them. 'What happened then, Jeremy?'

He began to smile. A reaching expression, stretching across his face. She began to understand why. They were back to this again. *Why don't you ask what you really want to know?* Maybe he'd maneuvered her back to it, or maybe she would always have come to this question in the end. To asking it so breathlessly, with so much anticipation. It wasn't her job to determine what happened to the dead boys. That was for the police, the Courts, the Coroner. She was here for the one boy who had walked out of there still living. The only witness. The only suspect. It was her job to assess his mental state for the Courts, which wasn't looking good.

Yet he was right. Just like everyone else, what she really wanted to know was what had happened to those dead, drowned, dried-out boys.

'They tied my shirt around my face,' he said and now he was full of detail. 'Held me down as they ripped it off me and tied it over my head. Then they started pouring water on it. On my face. I tried to fight them. I tried, but they laughed. I could hear them laughing.'

'Bullies will do that.'

'Aren't you going to ask why they were bullying me?'

She swallowed back the feeling of sand. 'Okay. Why?'

The corner of his mouth flicked up again. 'Bullies pick on the vulnerable. Isn't that what you're meant to say?' he said, too knowing. 'And then you're meant to tell me, in those all-so-gentle tones, that it doesn't get any more vulnerable than a kid who found his father dead at Christmas. Am I right?'

She shifted in her chair. 'Such things are true,' she said. It sounded like a protest. A weak one.

'Yeah, well it makes no fucking difference either way. They'd been threatening it for weeks. They were at me every other day, but no-one ever tried to stop them. And now it's too late.'

'Too late for the dead boys?'

'Too late for this whole fucking city. Nobody else was going to stop those fuckers, so I had to. I had to save myself somehow,' he said, with stiff shoulders, clenched jaw. 'Even though I knew. After Dad, I knew what it would mean. That there'd be no stopping it this time. That it'd build and build and build. But fuck it. I had to do it.'

'Jeremy, what did you do?'

'I did as they wanted. I brought the rain.'

He laughed. She let out a quick breath, only realising in that moment she'd been holding it.

The door flung open with a bang.

She jumped so high it felt like three layers of skin were ripped from her legs, left behind on the chair's sweaty leather. Found herself suddenly standing with her hands on her desk, drawing in quick breaths of hot air, the adrenaline kicking in to shake her from the inside out. It took her a moment to grab back control of her thoughts and her limbs, to push herself to stand straight and force her face into something vaguely professional.

Jeremy was grinning. In the doorway, Sally stood frowning at the spectacle she'd just made of herself.

'Yes, Sally. What is it?'

'You've gone over time. Jeremy's case worker is here to pick him up. She would like to know how much longer you'll be. Didn't you hear me knocking?'

She glanced at the wall clock. Shit. No wonder Sally looked unimpressed. She had gone so far into the next session's booking time they were practically through to the one after. Sally would have been the one apologising, rescheduling clients. Telling them this had never happened before. And it hadn't. She was always careful of the clock. It was part of her business. Sometimes it was necessary to stretch a session, it was unprofessional to shove someone out the door when in the midst of emotional outpouring, but she never let it go by so much and never without deliberate decision.

Her eyes flicked down to Jeremy, a dark smirk on his face.

'Thank you, Sally. We'll finish up now and be out shortly.'

Sally nodded, backing out of the room and clicking the door shut behind her. She waited until the receptionist was gone, until the silence had resumed.

Still standing, still trying to get her breath and her thoughts back into some kind of order.

She looked back down at Jeremy. She should say they needed to wrap up, suggest another appointment. Suggest, gently, that she would be advising the Court he needed immediate and regular medical attention, be prescribed the appropriate drugs, possibly a stay in hospital.

The moment she met the challenge in his stare, her carefully planned words evaporated.

'What happened in the toilet block, Jeremy?'

The question was out of her mouth before she had a chance to stop herself. Her voice sounded hoarse, strained words formed with a tacky tongue. The only reaction he gave was a slight raise of his eyebrows.

'Okay, Doc. If you like,' he said and his voice was clear. 'Davy and his mates said I was crazy. Scared-of-water and crazy. But they never checked where the water they were pouring on me was coming from.' He paused. 'Stupid bastards. I'd fucked up the taps in there already. I'd busted the pipes. There was no water to those bathrooms.'

'That's vandalism...'

'That's survival. They'd been threatening to do it to me for weeks. And nobody was going to help me.'

He stood up. It was a slow unravelling of limbs on the other side of her desk, until he met her eye to eye. He was tall when standing. A lanky sixteen year old, thin and towering. As tall as her. Taller. He leant forward and put his hands on the desk. He shoved his face suddenly close to hers and she tried not to back off, but couldn't help the flinch or the automatic step away. Her calves hit against the chair and she flopped back onto the leather surface.

'The human body. A good forty litres there, Doc. Just ripe for the harvest,' he said, his face too close, his

5,575.25+
1175.2
6750.45
Battle of Hastings
England - 1066
a) What King ruled at
b) What sides we

angry eyes all she could see. 'I made it rain. Just like they wanted. I made it rain and now it can't be stopped.'

'Jeremy...'

'The dead. They're thirsty. They need it to rain so bad.'

'Jeremy!'

He slammed both his hands down against her desk. She cried out through her dried-out throat, jolting backwards. She stared at him, his face a contortion of pain and distress. The kid nobody would help. Not his parents, not his school, not the authorities. Not her.

'I had to do it. They would have fucking drowned me,' he cried at her. 'My Christmas present to this shitty city I never wanted to be in. So you can all stop complaining about your water restrictions and your brown lawns and not being able to fill your fucking swimming pools.'

She clutched at the edge of her desk. Feeling for the alert button wired just below the lip, a signal to reception if she needed assistance. It was an insurance requirement; at least half her patients were referred from the courts. She had never used it before. She prided herself on being able to calm even the most agitated.

She pressed it several times.

'It's coming just in time for Christmas, Doc,' he said as she hit the alert button over and over again. 'This year, everybody's Christmas is going to be as fucked up as mine.'

The door swung open. Sally rushed through. No disapproval this time, just concern. Behind her was another woman. Young, flame-haired, quirky green summer suit. The social worker. The moment they entered, Jeremy pulled back. Glanced over his shoulder to see the women coming in, snorted derision.

Still behind her desk, she felt the breath go out of her. Her knees wanted to buckle. She sank, shaking, to her chair.

'Sally. Yes. Hello. We're done here,' she managed to say, her voice as shaky as her legs. 'We're done.'

The social worker surveyed the scene with narrowed eyes before turning to the teenager. He was standing calmly now, a mild expression on his face. Shoulders back, no slouch. When the social worker turned to him, he gave her a friendly smile.

'I hope you didn't screw up here, Jeremy,' the woman said. 'This is your last chance, remember.'

Jeremy only shrugged. He looked happy enough. There was a fluidity to the movement of his gangly teenage limbs. The woman turned her back on him, her mouth a tight line.

'Is all okay, Doctor?'

'Yes. Yes, it's okay,' she heard herself say.

'Do you need more time? I can stay if you need to extend the session further.'

But she shook her head. She needed no more. 'Thank you. I have enough.' She took a breath, pulled herself together. 'Thank you. I... I'll have my assessment to the Court by Monday. You'd like a copy yourself? For the file..?'

The social worker nodded that she would. There was curiosity in the woman's eyes. No doubt she was used to dealing with Jeremy and his sullen scowls. Not that he was scowling now or even looking all that sullen. Rather, he was standing with hands in the pockets of his jacket, head up, back straight. Gone was the alienated hunch, the cynical sneer at the world. He had even pushed the hair back out of his face, tucked it behind his ears. It made a lot of difference. His eyes were green, his face expressive, open. Friendly, even.

He looked, suddenly, like the boy in the photograph on the file. The one from eighteen months ago, back in the country, back in happier times.

'I can tell you what's in the report, if you want, Geraldine,' Jeremy said and even his voice was different. No growl, no cynicism. No attitude. He sounded relaxed.

Geraldine only half turned. 'Jeremy, let's just go.'

'No, really. It's not so hard,' he said. 'Damaged teenage boy, classic dysfunctional background. Mother undiagnosed alcoholic. Father clinically depressed, eventual suicide.'

He looked at them each in turn, meeting eyes without any challenge in his own. Just with a nod and a smile to assure them that yes, he was right on this. He knew it and they knew it.

'Shows signs of guilt, self-blame over father's suicide,' he said. Then he looked straight at her, sitting safe behind her desk. 'Victim of bullying following disruptive move away from familiar home environment. Reports hearing voices. Shows signs of paranoia, delusion. Further assessment needed to reach firm diagnosis. Schizophrenia, borderline-personality disorder or PTSD all possible. Recommend immediate psychiatric counselling, anti-psychotic medication, hospitalisation.'

He stopped. Let a beat of silence pass. Then cocked his head at her. 'Ain't that right, Doc?'

And it clicked. Suddenly, as she sat and stared at him. He'd been playing her. All along. Like the straight Cs so obviously engineered at school, it was an act. The troubled teenager act. Every scowl, every jaded tone, every sarcastic comment. Even the outfit, the black boots too heavy for the weather, the dyed hair only recently done. All that classic adolescent alienation, the vulnerability, the aggression. All carefully chosen and selected.

A construct. All designed to lead her to this exact point.

For what choice did she have but to go along with it? She could only report what she had seen and heard. What had happened in the room, up to and including why she had hit the alert.

'Yes, Jeremy,' she said, because she had to say something, because there was nothing else to say. 'That's about right.'

She sat there as Sally began to shift, taking the lead to show the social worker out of the room. Jeremy turned to follow obediently behind. He only looked back once and when he did it was with a flicker of a smile. A friendly, open smile that seemed only natural to his face, as he paused in the doorway and looked back with a wave of farewell.

He winked at her. 'Merry Christmas, Doc.'

She did not return the expression.

When they were gone and she was left behind her desk, sticky in the oppressive heat and silence, she closed her notebook. After a moment, she pushed it and the boy's file carefully to the middle of her desk. She wondered if the social worker, Geraldine, had figured him out. If his school had. If the Magistrate had. Right now, she was willing to bet if Jeremy hadn't outed himself there at the end, she wouldn't have clued into what he was really doing, either.

It wasn't that he had tricked her which bothered her. It was the reasons why.

Why would a kid as dangerously smart as he was choose to manipulate a deliberate diagnosis of trauma-induced psychosis?

The reason was as veiled as what had really gone on in that high school toilet block. Except now he would have an official expert assessment positioning him as *victim,* rather than *perpetrator*. Three dead and the only witness officially deemed unreliable, due to reasons of professionally diagnosed insanity.

After a while of sitting in the silence and the heat, she stood, began to move on automatic. Decided to cancel her appointments for the rest of the afternoon. The air conditioning mechanic couldn't come until the morning and it was too stifling in the office now to see anyone else. It was hard to breathe in here, with the heat filling all available space. Instead, she would push Jeremy out of her mind by doing something fun, something Christmas. Even completing her presents shopping would be enough. She would not write the assessment tonight, she would leave that for a day or two. Until she'd had a chance to process everything. Until she could get the kid and his Christmas out of her head.

She looked down at the little plastic tree. Could not help but think of Jeremy as she did.

The window was still open. She walked over to shut it, but found herself stopping, staring out into the bleached street beyond. The sun a power from overhead, washing out the landscape, draining everything of colour and energy. It was meant to be forty degrees today, according to the forecasts. She would have guessed it higher. Christmas day itself was forecast to be forty-three.

She looked up to the sky. A uniform blue. Not a cloud in it. Not a hope. It made her shudder. She shut the window and turned away.

She grabbed her handbag, her keys, her laptop in its case. Gathered her things, little sounds making empty echoes across her office. She slipped off the uncomfortable, sweaty heels and slipped on some light canvas walking shoes fished out of her bottom-drawer.

Everything about her felt damp, sweaty. Only her throat felt dry, her mouth, her tongue. No saliva, no moisture. She was so thirsty. So damn thirsty.

She tried not to think of tales of the thirsty dead and reached instead for the glass of water on her desk. Beside the little Christmas tree, beside the boy's file. She even got so far as to raise it to her mouth.

She stopped it there.

She could almost feel the cool, clear liquid at her lips.

When she put it back down again, back in the middle of the desk, it was on top of the file. Jeremy's file. Jeremy's glass. The same one she had seen him drink until it was empty. She had seen him swallow every last drop.

She heard her own breath, a wheeze in her dried throat. So hard to breathe through it, hard to stretch her lips, her throat and mouth too dried out, her stomach twisting with the thirst. And then she heard behind her a soft, fat splat. Followed by another. Then more. It became a kind of patter. She twisted, turning to stare at the window.

Outside, it was beginning to rain.

GLITTERING WERE THE LEAVES

TONY DEWS

My name's Curtis and I'm not here anymore. Well I am still here, but by the time you're reading this I most likely won't be. I'll be somewhere but that's all I can be sure of since my here and your here aren't the same anymore, or won't be. I don't even know where here is or where it will be, no idea at all. In fact if you wanted to be facetious you could say I'm neither here nor there. Wherever here or there is. I used to think that the world was rational like you and everybody else but not anymore. What you see and what you know, and what I saw and what I knew aren't the whole story, you see. There's more to the world than you imagine. Quite a lot more in fact. Some of it is good and some of it isn't quite so good and some of it is dangerous, and maybe evil. Some is dark and some is brilliant. I guess I'd better start at the beginning so you know where I'm coming from. Even if, like me, you have no idea where I'm going. Don't worry if you find it unbelievable. If it wasn't happening to me I probably wouldn't believe it either. It would just be a story.

*****

I was hunting through the antique shops and little flea markets in Fitzroy, looking for stuff to put in my new place in Clifton Hill, since I'd decided to renovate and refurbish it bit by bit. I had certain things in mind of course, stuff that wouldn't only fit but would look just right; period pieces, the modern stuff looks way too sterile to me, no soul, no character. All that stuff you feel in a terrace area like the one I'd moved into. Wood does it for me; not plastic, metal and glass. The house does it for me too. A two-storey place just off Queen's Parade that hadn't been gutted in the chase for that modern feel. Though why people buy an old terrace house and then turn it into a glass and chrome temple is beyond me. It was near work too.

I was in this shop just up from Smith St on Gertrude St, big place full of clothes and books as well as furniture when I got to chatting to the owner. Getting to know the owners of places bears fruit in so many ways. You can not only get a better price but they get to know your likes and dislikes and can keep an eye out for something you might be interested in so you get a chance to buy it before anyone else sees it. I've picked some good stuff over the years this way. Besides, I like a chat. It was an older bloke who ran this place, in his fifties, wearing a frayed vest, balding and showing the signs of a life well lived. He was a nice guy, and he knew his stuff, that's for sure.

“Can I help you at all?”

I was eyeing off a welsh dresser when he asked me. “Yeah maybe you can. I've just got a place in Clifton

Hill and I'm looking to refurnish and refurbish it a bit. You seem to have a few things that would look good in the place."

He looked at me and then at the dresser I had sort of casually rested my hand on in a manner that said I was interested but not too interested. "I see. Well that dresser certainly will do the job for you there. It dates from the late nineteenth century and is made of jarrah. It still looks good too. Great workmanship. This piece will last for ages yet." He ran his hands over it like a beau would run his hands over a woman. "Great buy for a discerning man like you." Charmer. He looked like a man who, if he sold it, would lose his soul and happily count the cash at the same time.

I looked at the price, handwritten on a tag attached to handle of a drawer, $1499. Not bad if you have a high disposable income. "Do you deliver?"

And that's how I ended up with an antique dresser in the living room. It fitted as snug as anything, like it was built to fit just there. I just stood there for a while looking at it and enjoying the feeling you get when you buy something and you know it's just right. Beautiful. After dinner –microwaved, did I say I was single? – I sat there with a bottle of red and slowly drank it, basking in how the wood reflected the light. A deep brown with gold highlights when the light hit it just so, it looked terrific but somehow I got the feeling I should move it over to the side wall so people could see and enjoy it when they walked in the room. Not tonight though, it was Sunday tomorrow and I'd have all day.

The next day was a typical Melbourne autumn day. A cold, sunny morning that made you want to sit outside at a café with a latté and the paper, just feeling glad to be alive. So I did and if I'd known what was going to happen I would've stayed there all day and left the dresser where it was. Or taken it back with some excuse why it wasn't right when I'd tried to find a spot for it. I guess that's the problem with second guessing yourself. You just end up chasing your metaphorical tail until you disappear up your own logical orifice. What's done is done. We make our decisions and live with the consequences for good or ill and nothing can be done to change things.

Like I said, the dresser was jarrah, solid and heavy. Too heavy by far for a skinny bloke like me to move it without a bit of effort. So I took the drawers out and the doors off so I could get a grip on it enough to wiggle and shuffle it over the floorboards in a kind of drunkard's walk. It took a while but I got it there in the end. It was when I was putting the drawers back in that I noticed one was shallower than the others. Not by much, just a finger width or so, so it was almost unnoticeable. The base was the same wood as the others to disguise it to anything other than a hard look or blind chance. Certainly a quick glance would've normally missed it.

It was intriguing, that's for sure. Who'd done it and why go to the trouble? Curiosity may kill the cat but I wanted to check it out. I tapped it a few times with a screwdriver to find out if it was solid or hollow. It was hollow but some of it had a dead, flat sound like there was something in there. Not big. About the size of a notebook, and whoever had hidden it in there sure wanted to make it hard to find.

It took a bit of fiddling to remove the false bottom. I didn't want to damage the drawer and I didn't have a lot of tools to help me do it but eventually I succeeded with a few splinters in my fingers as trophies. Underneath the false bottom was a book, a notebook and it looked to be nearly as old as the dresser. The cover was blue leather, faded in spots, and bound by a thin strip of the same leather. The pages were yellowed and the ink faded but it was still readable. It looked like a journal, handwritten with no title and no name just initials; J.L.

I put it down on the coffee table and stared at it for a while. I felt like an intruder with access to the most private hidden thoughts of another person. Was I fated to find the book? No, that's not the right word really, better to say now with hindsight that I was doomed to find it. I picked it up and started to read.

To whom it may concern,

If perchance you are reading this journal then I have been singularly unsuccessful in hiding it well enough to ensure it would avoid detection. I fear that I have not long to go in this world and I pray that I can finish it before my end as we know it arrives. Whilst you are reading this you may consider me mad at worst or deluded at best and the merciful God above knows I have oft doubted my own sanity these past months wherein I have discerned another reality. One which, oh dear God, seeks me to join it.

Not a bad way to start a story, I thought. It must have been one after all and not a journal. Nothing like that could be true, could it? It did sound a tad clichéd, but they used a different English style in those days after all. I kept reading though. It was interesting to say the least, until I went to bed. The journal wasn't long and there were gaps of days here and there as I flicked through it. He was obviously not a guy to write every day. The date of the first entry was May 3rd, 1904. Today's date.

It was a normal day when I awoke this morning. All seemed the same as it was yesterday and the days before that. I heard the clinking of bottles as the milkman went about his morning rounds and the sounds of the awakening city were all about me as I prepared myself for my day's work. I certainly was not in any ways ready for what was about to befall me and I surely doubt any man would have been anything other than similarly disposed, being that it would be beyond anyone's ken. As I caught the tram which would take me to my employment in the city, I noticed out of the corner of my eye that the leaves on the trees were glittering silver. They reminded me of Christmas decorations that shift and shiver when the breeze catches them. I first believed this to be a mere trick of the early morning light, one I had not noticed before. Alas I was soon disabused of this notion when I saw that all the leaves on all the trees I saw that morning were likewise glittering silver.

May 6th, 1904.

The leaves are still that shade of silver. I have started to become used to this strange state of affairs as well as the fact that everyone else appears not to have noticed this singular phenomenon. As to why this is the case I have no idea so I have resolved to

> *mention it not and observe what I can should anything else occur. Needless to say that this being the case, I have not tried too hard to convince my work colleagues and my peers nor anyone else lest I be confined to a sanatorium for my own well-being. Nothing else seems untoward that I have noticed so I will manage as best I can in order to manage my own sanity. Perhaps it is just as well that only I can see the silver leaves.*

I decided to scour the internet to get any idea of who J.L. was. Maybe I wasn't reading a journal but the first draft of a book. So I hunted around to see if anything had been published around that time that had used what I had read as a plot. No luck and, believe me, I looked hard. There was no mention of an author with those initials who had written at that time, not even a short story. That wasn't a bad thing of course. An unknown manuscript could be worth a bit, but without knowing who the author was I'd be struggling to get much for it. Still, it was an option for later. I could look into that after I'd finished reading it.

First I thought to read a page a day or at least an entry a day. The only snag was that he often left gaps of a few days to just over a week. So I decided to read each entry on the day it was written. It seemed to be kind of respectful to the writer to do it that way. And it focussed me too, I only had to make myself stick to my plan. Given the future it was probably good for me to read it that way.

May 11th, 1904.

I do not notice the colour of the leaves now, nor do I pay more than scant attention to the different colours of the flowers I see about me which is a more recent development. When I saw this a few days ago it scarce surprised me nor was it concerning. If indeed it is the case that I am losing my mind then the different colours of the flowers are a most benign case of this. It is certainly better than descending into the most slavering hell of lunacy which fills all reasonable men with fear. But there was something different this day, something which gives me no small measure of foreboding. You see I saw, or thought I in some sense perceived, something out of the corner of my eye. It was a shape or perhaps a shadow flickering and shifting and yet, when I cast my gaze to the spot where I saw this form I could see nothing. The leaves and flowers affected naught but my vision but this fleeting vision of something I could not see caused the very hairs on the back of my neck to rise and a frisson of fear to tickle my heart. I do not know what it was but the mere possibility I will soon find out is not a prospect I savour.

I have to admit that when I put the journal down after reading that last entry it was a weird feeling that came over me. I've grown up like most in my generation with movies like *Dawn of the Dead* and *Resident Evil* but that last bit gave me the creeps a bit that's for sure. It was a good read and I did look at the shadows cast through the window by the trees outside. Nothing there of course, it's just a story I was reading. But all the same, stories like this have their place in our time of reason and rationality and 'it's the economy stupid' mantra we live by. If it had been printed I think it would have been a best-seller and come to think of it, it still could be. I wondered idly what it would have been like for someone to actually see this happen. What would they go through? How would they cope with going to work while this was happening to them and then coming home and writing it all down? It wasn't something I'd like to go through.

May 13th, 1904.

I call them shadows for such they seem to be. They are here still, perhaps more numerous than when I first noticed them, yet still difficult to see. They lurk in the dark corners and the in-between places where we do not normally look and so they are hard to perceive. Perhaps they have always been there, dismissed as flights of fancy if we do notice them, mentally shooing them away as we do to a troublesome fly seeking to sup at our sweat. As I sit each night I oft times think that they are all around me and everyone else but that surely cannot be the case. I am after all a rational man and I know that nonesuch can be the case. I am avowed to seek a rational, scientific explanation for these visions else my very world may surely cease.

The book stopped for a while then. Several days went by until the next entry. I was more certain it was fiction, a journal would have to have something every day, that's what they're for. Or so I'm told that is, never felt the need to keep one myself. I'm way too ordinary. Still if it was real I had to wonder what was happening. Were the shadows still there? How was the poor bastard feeling? But I had to wait until the day of the next entry to find out. In the meantime I went to work, socialised, caught up with friends. All was normal and all the while the journal sat on the table, looking at me and daring me to look at it again.

May 17th, 1904.

They, the shadows, are ever more numerous, even though they still remain affixed to the edges of my vision, only to vanish like smoke in the wind when I turn to face the places they appear within. It is indeed a most singular sensation to see something you know others do not. Furthermore, despite my searchings I have found nothing in any literature that can ascribe any kind of reality to what I am observing each day and night – for indeed they must be in the night also, I have no doubt of that even though I cannot see them. There may even be more of them between dusk and dawn as there are more places they can take refuge from being seen. Ah but hearken to me, discussing these figments of my imagination as if they are real; entities that can think, hide and even behave as if alive. I am not quite delusional here as people speak of animals and pets in much the same way, ascribing to them in their naivety human motivations and feelings they do not possibly possess. Perhaps I am doing this in order to explain what I am seeing where no other method will suffice. Or perhaps I am not.

Silver leaves and dark shadows lurking at the edges of vision. You'd think that wouldn't be scary these days but like I said it was certainly getting to me. I'd given up on finding a buyer for the manuscript and now I reckoned it would be better published and I was going to look around the publishers to see who would pick it up. It would need some work of course, better characterisation and a setting needed to be done among others, but the basics were there. It was hard to keep to my reading plan but I had to respect the book and the writer. Mind you, I have to admit the temptation to read ahead to the ending was almost too much to bear.

May 20th, 1904.

Today I have seen one of the shadows for the first time in its totality. I believe I must be getting better at seeing and focussing my gaze when I notice them because on this occasion I was too fast for it. My gaze captured it as easily as a net captures a fish. It was black, so black as to appear blue in places when it moved. It was small, and although it was humanoid in shape it was almost amorphous, sinuous perhaps, seeming to stretch and shift enough for me to initially doubt it's human shape. It neither walked nor glided, seeming instead to have a means of locomotion that lay in between the two.

The shadow was about the size of a child of five years I would say, certainly no larger. Interestingly, even though I saw the apparition about noon, moving down a lane way near my residence, it cast no shadow and though I first believed them to be shadows at first I now believe this is not the case. Unlike a shadow which is merely the result of some solid object blocking light, it was as if this being, if such a word suffices, absorbed light, such was its ebony shade. I was in some odd sense glad of my chance observation as I could now see they appeared to have a physical presence, and in knowing this I could resume my searching for an explanation of their existence. I resumed my search without delay.

May 26th, 1904.

Alas I must confess that my searching, as before, has been fruitless. Not a mention of these shadows can be found anywhere that I have looked in the areas of natural history and psychology. I fear I might have to search more esoteric writings but this is surely nonsense. They are obviously physical in nature and do not belong in any manner of writing that deals with the supernatural. They are noticeably more numerous now and, perhaps emboldened by my inability to do anything about them other than observe, they wander quite freely in my presence. I am quite unable to sense any purpose in what they are doing but doubtless there must be one. Ah if only that was clear to me.

Then nothing. No entry for nearly a month. What did the writer see? No not the writer, the poor bastard facing what he was in the imagination of J.L. Not a hint, not a sentence, not a word. Just silence.

June 20th, 1904.

The leaves are all silver now and so are all the flowers; the dandelions, roses and native flora are all of the one gleaming silver shade. The very sky itself is likewise changed, for instead of different shades of blue with clouds passing overhead, it is now a gleaming silver-blue with not a cloud to break its burnished metallic glow. Nor have I seen nor felt any rain for a fortnight at least, and yet rain does occur. I see the other people carrying their umbrellas and unfurling and furling them in turn and jumping or sidestepping puddles that I neither see nor feel. I see them also constellating under shop awnings as best they can while I walk by untouched by any precipitation. The God above only knows what they must think as they see me pass by like some apparition or wild creature wandering the streets.

June 21st, 1904.

I have lost my employment. I have no qualms about this and I will cope readily enough. Most people appear not to notice me as I walk the streets and I will gain sustenance easily enough though no doubt some would think my means abhorrent. Such time as I have remaining, and I fear this might not be much, I will spend as fruitfully as feasible in searching for the answer I have yet to find and yet which must also exist. I seek not for myself of course but for whatever poor soul may find this document, even though I have vowed to hide it as securely as possible. If someone does find it I hope they gain some understanding of what is occurring to me. I can only hope. The behaviour of the shades seems to have revealed at last some purpose to their movements. Patterns and reason appears to be emerging. I must observe more before it is too late. Mayhap the fate of another may be averted or altered if I am able to so do.

June 24th, 1904.

My observations have confirmed my last entry. The beings, for such they are in having their own corporeality, stop and watch as people walk past them unknowingly. It appears as if they are waiting, I am not sure for what as yet, but I have a suspicion – and it is no more than this – that they are waiting for death. Not theirs it seems to me but of some unsuspecting soul, someone they wait for to take them to perdition itself. Perhaps this is no more than a suspicion as I said, for I have not seen anything that needs must would confirm it, but I fear it to be the truth. I hope most fervently that I never find out, for the confrontation in my mind would surely drive me out of my wits.

June 28th, 1904.

I have sensed a changing in my surrounds today and I fear the consequences for my mental and physical well-being. The beings watch me now as I pass, however they do not follow me like they do others before accompanying them on what I am now certain is to be their final journey. It is as if they know a different fate awaits me, one they can take no part in. The world has taken to a kind of shimmering and I sense there is something about to break through to replace it, one that I and none other will be a part of. People around me are also becoming vague to my sight as if they are not fully there like hallucinations or dreams. They, or perhaps it is I, are about to vanish as would an illusionist's assistant behind a veil.

July 4th, 1904.

This is perhaps to be my last entry. For some few days now I have been able to see through people and buildings and on occasions been able to pass through each unhindered and unobserved. I confess I was shaken to my core when such first occurred but now I almost rejoice in it. The world of silver and metal gleam that lies behind what we take for granted as the one reality has become more and more real to me. Indeed I seem to walk in that world more than in the world of men in which I must appear as a phantom, a ghost; ephemeral, appearing perhaps as a fleeting

> *shadow. I now belong to the world that is coming to take me but why it does so I cannot say. Perhaps answers will come to me there, I wait to find out the truth of that. The pen is even now slipping through my grasp like oil, it takes all my effort and will to maintain a grip on it sufficient to write these final words. I have readied a place for this journal so that it may remain hidden from the sight of men and my last act will be to place it there. Farewell.*

The book ended there. After I put the book down I searched the dresser to see if anything else had been placed in there under a false bottom or a false back but no luck. This was all there was. Pity really, it would have been nice to have known a bit more. Before I go though I will say only one thing. If you're reading this, stop. Burn it, bury it, do whatever you like but make sure you do it properly and make sure nobody else can read it. Words have power but I hadn't realised just how much power they have until just now. I thought this was only a story without a writer waiting for someone to find it and get it published or a failed first attempt at a book that had been tossed away. But it isn't, not by a long way. If you want to know why, here it is. I just looked through the window of the front room and the leaves, dear God the leaves were glittering silver

auslit.net

The Australian Literature Review

INTERVIEW WITH GORDON REECE WHICH APPEARED ON THE AUSTRALIAN LITERATURE REVIEW WEBSITE IN DECEMBER 2011:

Your short story Ho Ho Ho was the inspiration for the *Ho Ho Horror* anthology. How did you come to write Ho Ho Ho?

I found the Australian bush an inspiring place for horror fiction – the small town settings, the isolation, a landscape that can feel dangerous and threatening - and I wanted to write a series of horror short stories set in the fictional town of Jemimaville in North East Victoria. 'Ho, ho, ho' is the first short story I've done and the second one, 'Carneval (sic)', is almost finished. The idea would be that characters from one story would appear fleetingly in the other stories, so a story, say, about Jemimaville's doctor might start with him treating Danny Coyle, the main protagonist of 'Ho, ho, ho'.

What can readers look forward to in Ho Ho Ho?

When I've sent 'Ho, ho, ho' to friends I've normally added a health warning along the lines of 'this is a nasty story – you've been warned!' I think it's the ending that particularly freaks people out – anything to do with eyes is a hard one (I still can't watch the eye scene in 'Un

Chien Andalou'). It's a bit of a comic satire on doting parents and spoilt children I guess too. Lieutenant Danger is based on 'Captain Scarlet', from the Gerry Anderson ('Thunderbirds') series, which I used to love as a kid and still do – I bought the whole series on DVD in Melbourne last year. I also used to have an Action Man and would to drop him out of my bedroom window – but there (I hope) any similarities between me and Danny end!

Both Ho Ho Ho and your novel *Mice* feature violence and psychological disturbance. What do you think makes these kinds of stories appeal to readers, or what appeals to you about writing these kinds of stories?

When other kids were reading Enid Blyton, 'Treasure Island', and 'Swallows and Amazons', I was reading American horror comics. They were gory and violent and full of delicious black humour and irony. I enjoyed the shock and the power of these comics, the melodramatic hyperbole, the extreme plots, the unexpected twist endings, and I suppose they established the paradigm for the type of story I wanted to write. What I've learnt over the years is that you can use the horror/thriller genre to explore serious issues and that, ironically, it's by looking in very dark places that we can shed the most light on the human condition. Arguably, that's what Shakespeare did – 'Macbeth' (murder), 'Othello' (jealousy), 'Hamlet' (revenge) – characters in extremis, characters buckling and bending out of shape under extraordinary stress, that's where you find the real meat in the sandwich.

What are some of your favourite horror stories, and what makes them work so well for you as a reader?

I would say my stand out horror stories would be 'The Monkey's Paw' (W.W. Jacobs), 'Green Fingers' (RC Cook), Poe's 'The Tell-Tale Heart' and 'The Cask of Amontillado', Graham Greene's 'Proof Positive' and 'The End of the Party' and Maupassant's 'The Hand' and 'A Vendetta'. Each story has a 'gory' element, but they have something else which is more important. You could call it 'the chill factor' – Major Weaver talking in tongues and drumming his fingers on the table before collapsing dead in 'Proof Positive', or the widow Saverini feeding her lean black dog 'something brown' as she returns home after the murder in 'A Vendetta'. It's the little details that make the flesh creep that embed a really good horror story in the mind. I read 'Green Fingers' once when I was a kid and I haven't read it since, but I've never forgotten the image of the naked old woman growing slowly up out of the soil in the back garden like some hideous shrub.

You recently toured the US for *Mice*. What was that experience like for you?

I wish it had been a tour of the US, maybe that will come later. I actually just spent a week in New York and did a podcast and a radio interview. The US publication is hugely important for any book and I was chuffed to get good reviews in The New Yorker magazine and the New

York Times. Now 'Mice' has been optioned by Groundswell, the US movie production company, I think its profile will grow in the US – especially when the director has been assigned and the two female leads have been cast. I am very pleased 'Mice' is in Groundswell's hands now – Groundswell made the movie 'Sideways' which is one of my all-time favourites.

What advice would you like to offer for writers starting their first novel manuscript?

I suppose patience is one of the most important things for a new writer to have – I had to wait seven years for 'Mice' to be published. Along with patience you need persistence; you have to keep on going even after receiving a million rejection slips. The fact is that you could write the greatest novel ever written and publishers will still return it saying 'sorry, we do not read unsolicited manuscripts.' I would also advise new writers to think commercially. There are great opportunities now in genre fiction – the world never tires of detective stories – and once you've made money with five novels about your hard-bitten gumshoe you can then write your 'War and Peace'. I think you have to box clever, look where the trends are (eg crossover novels) and see if you can't make a name there – no one says you have to do that forever, but getting a start is so hard it's smart to try to level the playing field a bit. Never forget the Dr Johnson quote: 'No man but a blockhead ever wrote, except for money.'

If you could bring one storyteller back from the dead for a day for the sole purpose of talking to them about writing fiction, who would it be and why?

That's a tough one. Tolstoy would definitely be on the list as would Graham Greene, but I think George Orwell would be my first choice. Orwell's output was amazingly varied; he wrote 'traditional' novels ('Burmese Days'), memoir ('A Homage to Catalonia'), political allegory/children's fiction ('Animal Farm'), science fiction ('1984'), comedy ('Keep the Aspidistra Flying'), and campaigning journalism in the tradition of Dickens ('The Road to Wigan Pier'), so, although maybe not as naturally gifted as Tolstoy or Greene, he was the consummate writer, experimenting in an assortment of genres that required different techniques and aesthetics. I think the variety of his literary output plus his idiosyncratic mind and brutal honesty would afford some amazing insights into the writing process.

What is next for your fiction writing?

I'm writing an adult novella called 'The Dentist' at the moment, a thriller/horror set in the UK in the 1950s. When I've finished that I'll return to my Jemimaville stories and the new young adult novel for Allen and Unwin. I'd like to write for cinema and am half way through a script writing course at the moment. Script writing is very different to prose writing, and although the actual writing is easier, figuring out the best way to present your story *visually* is actually very hard!

www.ingramcontent.com/pod-product-compliance
Lightning Source LLC
LaVergne TN
LVHW010913110826
845149LV00013B/2345

* 9 7 8 0 9 8 7 1 2 4 2 2 7 *